THE MAN
WITH THE
RED
BAG

OTHER NOVELS
BY EVE BUNTING

THE MAN WITH THE

RED
BAG

Eve Bunting

Joanna Cotler Books
An imprint of HarperCollins*Publishers*

The Man with the Red Bag

Copyright © 2007 by Edward D. Bunting and Anne E. Bunting,

Trustees of the Edward D. Bunting and Anne E. Bunting Family Trust

For information address HarperCollins Children's Books, a division of HarperCollins Publishers,

1350 Avenue of the Americas, New York, NY 10019.

www.harpercollinschildrens.com

Library of Congress Cataloging-in-Publication Data.

Bunting, Eve

The man with the red bag / Eve Bunting.—1st ed.

p.   cm.

Summary: In the months following the September 11, 2001 terrorist attacks, twelve-year-old
Kevin, an aspiring mystery writer traveling cross-country with his grandmother on a sightseeing
trip to various national parks and monuments, suspects a sinister-looking man in his tour group
of carrying a bomb.

ISBN 978-0-06-081828-9 (trade bdg.)

ISBN 978-0-06-081835-7 (lib. bdg.)

[1. Travel—Fiction.   2. Terrorism—Fiction.   3. Mystery and detective stories.]   I. Title.

PZ7.B91527Map 2007   2006103558

[Fic]—dc22

Typography by Neil Swaab

1 2 3 4 5 6 7 8 9 10

First Edition

For Ed, who travels with me all the way

—E.B.

THE MAN
WITH THE
RED
BAG

CHAPTER

1

I held the bag tight against me. If there was a bomb in here, it wouldn't be too smart to jiggle it.

Running, running.

Stavros's boots pounded on the path behind me.

"Hey! You've got my bag!" he yelled.

My heart thumped with fear.

And then he was beside me.

Right from the beginning I was suspicious of the man. Right from the minute he got on the bus. Maybe it was because he acted so strangely about the bag. But mostly it was because of the way he looked. And because my ears started tingling at the sight of him— an ancient warning of danger, not to be ignored.

Of course, at that time, at the beginning, my suspicions were just gut level. Well, it was June 20, 2002, not even a year after 9/11. That's a date no one will ever forget. September 11, 2001, when terrorists hijacked four planes and flew them into the towers of the World Trade Center in New York and into the Pentagon and that field somewhere in Pennsylvania. This guy looked like he might be Saudi Arabian or even Iraqian, if there is such a word. He was dark skinned, with bushy black eyebrows and a bushier mustache. So maybe it was natural for me to be on the alert. We were supposed to be. Even President Bush had said that on TV.

I could tell that I wasn't the only watchful one. There was a kind of rustling, a whispering from the other tour passengers, as he came through the bus door. I think that little 9/11 alarm bell was ringing for all of us. Of course, a bus isn't an airplane. But still, who knows what evil lurks in the hearts of men? And then there was the bag.

He was holding one of the dorky red carry-ons

the Star Tours Company had sent to each of us before the trip. It was awkward for him to carry because his right hand was bandaged, all the way from his fingertips to his wrist. Declan Taylor, our tour director, immediately reached for the bag as the man stepped up into the coach.

"Hi!" Declan said. "Let me get this for you."

But the man pulled the bag close to his chest and shook his head. "No, no," he said. "I'll keep it." The words were forceful. But the intense way he clutched the bag was really strange. As if he was afraid someone would try to take it from him.

Weird, I thought. What could he have in there? Maybe a bunch of money or stolen jewels? My ears tingled ferociously.

I hadn't seen the man before. He hadn't been at last night's "get-acquainted" dinner. Maybe he didn't want to get acquainted.

He scared me, and I decided I'd keep a wary eye on him.

I was actually glad to have something to think about during this trip, besides the passing scenery. Grandma and I were starting out on a "nostalgic journey."

Nostalgic for her, that is. We were going to see the Grand Tetons and Yellowstone Park in Wyoming and Mount Rushmore in South Dakota. My grandma had done this trip by car with my grandpa when they were first married. But Grandpa died last year, when I was only eleven, and we were all missing him so much. Especially Grandma.

"I want to go back and see it all again, Kevin," Grandma had told me. "Come with me," she'd said.

To be honest, I hadn't really wanted to go. It was the beginning of summer vacation. I could have been home in Los Angeles, skateboarding, shooting hoops, playing catch with the guys. My best buddy, Justin, and I had planned to camp out in my backyard. But I was here instead. There'd be a lot of sightseeing on this tour. I'm not much into sightseeing.

But my mom and dad had been all for it.

"You'll see parts of the country you've never seen before," Mom said.

"There'll be all kinds of wildlife, too," Dad added. "Moose and elk and deer and bears."

"Gnarly," I said, faking up my enthusiasm.

4

Mom stroked my hand. "It will be such a wonder-ful bonding experience for you and your grandma."

"We're already bonded," I told her. Not to be soppy, but I love my grandma a lot. She's fun. She listens when I talk to her. We both like old movies. She loves me a whole lot, too. And that's basically why I was here now.

"You'll bond even more," Mom said firmly.

Grandma had booked the ten-day trip way before 9/11. For a while after that we weren't sure if we should go. But one afternoon Gran had a long, serious talk with my parents. "I don't blame you for being worried," she told them. She offered to go alone.

"We think it's okay for him to go," Mom said. "But it's up to you, Kev."

I have to admit that for a couple minutes I was really tempted to use the big excuse Grandma had just given me and bail. But then I looked at her and I knew I wouldn't.

"Let's do it," I said.

We'd flown from L.A. to Salt Lake City.

In my Star Tours bag I'd brought my Walkman

and a bunch of CDs, my new Joan Lowery Nixon novel, my much-read how-to-write-a-mystery book, and my trusty notebook, in which I planned to write my very first mystery novel following the guidelines and instructions that I would read carefully as we tooled along in our big tour bus. Tucked in the bottom of my red bag was my square of blue blanket. That's all that's left of what was once in my baby crib. I know I'm twelve years old. I know I'm a boy. So what? I still sleep with it under my head at night. I'd definitely croak, of course, if any of my friends knew about it. They'd call me a wuss and worse. All of which makes it hard when I go on sleepovers, but I manage okay. I'm very dexterous, which means skillful.

So on day two of the tour, when the man got on the bus, things started looking up. Suddenly I had a project. I'd watch him, take notes, maybe get my whole book done, first draft, before we got home. Well, at least the first few chapters. And besides that, I'd be an anonymous, unpaid security guard for the tour. I'd be a bodyguard for Grandma.

I eyeballed him closely.

He was about my dad's age. His jeans had a neat

crease down each leg. His shirt was checked blue and white and he wore shiny leather cowboy boots. A windbreaker was draped over his right arm.

He sat in the first aisle seat, leaving the place by the window vacant except for the bag beside him. He wedged his windbreaker in at his side. I took a good look at the bandage on his right hand. It was white and bulky. He wouldn't be able to do much with that hand. With the other he clutched the handle of the red bag. He stared straight ahead. Every time I glanced across the aisle at him, my ears vibrated gently.

Our coach was more than half empty. Declan had told us last night that there'd been "several cancellations" on recent trips. More than several, I suspected. He'd explained it was because of 9/11. Lots of people were still scared to get on a plane. Declan said almost all of Star Tours' passengers had to fly to Salt Lake City, where the tour began, and the flying part had stopped them. "I have to congratulate those of you who decided to follow through on your plans," he added. "We can't let terrorists ruin our lives."

That's more or less what Mom and Dad and Grandma had said, too.

When Declan made that pronouncement, I felt incredibly brave.

I looked behind me at the other brave travelers. Some of them were studying the maps and itineraries that Declan had handed out last night. Most still wore their name tags. "There are just eighteen of us," he'd said. "We're going to be one big family for the next nine days. So let's get pally."

The reflection in my window showed me the guy right behind us—a tall, giraffe shape—and the girl with him, whose name was Geneva Jenson. She was thirteen. I knew because Grandma had asked last night. The man was her dad, though he was older than my dad or the dads of my friends.

"Hi," I'd said at the get-acquainted dinner, stoked that there was someone semi my age on the trip. I'd peered again at her name tag. "Geneva. That's really different."

"It's a town in Switzerland," she'd said.

"I know that." I'd managed not to sound irritated. Did she think I was that dumb?

"And don't ever call me Genny," she'd said. "I hate Genny."

8

"Okay, Genny. I'll remember. And my name's Kevin, but you can call me Mr. Saunders if you like." I grinned.

She'd grinned back. "Cool!"

We'd talked a bit more. She and her dad were from Washington, the state, not the D.C. one. I thought she was kind of pretty, with her tufty yellow hair and navy blue eyes. But I'm not much of a judge of "pretty."

Now I waved to her reflection in the window, and she waved back. Then I held my hand to the side of my mouth and whispered the way James Cagney does in old movies on TV. "That guy over there? With the bag?" I nodded in his direction. "Check him out!"

She glanced across, then raised her shoulders in a "what *about* him?" gesture.

"Later," I Cagney-whispered.

Declan had jumped off the bus to check that the luggage was properly stowed, but here he was, back again.

"And how is everyone this morning?" he asked. Declan was shrimp-small, young, and thin. He wore a great wide-brimmed cowboy hat, jeans, and a shirt that had red, white, and blue stripes, so bright they made you blink. I blinked. If we got off the coach for any reason we'd be able to find him pretty easily.

His voice boomed through the mike. "I have one introduction to make. The gentleman sitting behind Scotty, our driver, arrived last night from New York. His flight was late, so he missed the party. His name is Charles Stavros." Declan windmilled his arms and ordered, "Everyone: 'Good morning, Charles.'"

There was an enthusiastic response of "Good morning, Charles."

Charles took his good hand from the bag— reluctantly, I thought, but that was probably just my imagination at work. He waved.

"Stavros," Grandma whispered. "I think that's a Greek name." She smiled at me. "Can you hear the unanimous sigh of relief? They were half expecting Osama or Saddam. It's sad. People are so quick to jump to conclusions now. If someone looks like that—"

"No kidding," I said. But I knew I was disappointed. There went my mystery-adventure novel. On the other hand . . . I sat up straight and stared at him. How did we know that was his *real* name? He could *be* Osama, or Saddam. I wouldn't let myself be lulled into a false sense of security, no matter what Grandma said.

"Everybody ready to get under way?" Declan asked.

"Yes."

"Definitely."

"Let's bounce!" someone called.

"We's a-goin', we's a movin'," Declan chanted in a singsong voice.

I nonchalantly glanced again at Mr. Charles Stavros—just in time to see him lift his left hand, kiss his fingertips, and then make the sign of the cross over the red bag.

A shiver ran up my spine and my ears vibrated.

What on earth was *in* there?

As soon as we were moving, I opened my mystery notebook and wrote my title:

The Man with the Red Bag

I liked it. It was definitely grabby, which is very important in a mystery novel. Then I wrote:

Characters

I was going to have eighteen if I counted Declan. That was a lot. I chewed on the end of my pencil and wrote:

1. Mystery man, Charles Stavros. Maybe Greek, maybe not. What's with his red bag?

2. Geneva. Don't call her Genny.

3. Geneva's father. Where's her mother, by the way?

4. Bruce Dove <u>and</u>

5. Nellie Dove—husband and wife. Old, nice. They hold hands.

6. Beth Yokomata <u>and</u>

7. Millie Yokomata—sisters. Japanese American. Young and cute. Millie is definitely the bossy one.

8. Buffo Roberts <u>and</u>

9. Blessing Roberts—husband and wife. He's an ex-football player and he's huge. She's a beautician and she's huge, too. They have identical red, spiky hair.

10. Midge Ketchikan. Don't know much about her yet. She's about my grandma's age.

11. First Texan <u>and</u>

12. Second Texan <u>and</u>

13. Third Texan <u>and</u>

14. Fourth Texan—two men and two women. They're "pardners" and they stick together like burrs.

15. Grandma.

16. Declan—tour director.

17 Scotty—bus driver.

18. Kevin—me.

Too many. Some of them would have to be minor characters. I wouldn't spend much time on them.

Grandma was knitting a blue scarf for my dad. She peered out of the windows happily while her needles clickety-clacked and the blue yarn snaked up from the red bag at her feet.

"Knitting is very 'in' now," she told me. "It's not just for old ladies anymore."

"For old men?" I asked.

She nodded. "Why not?"

She didn't ask what I was writing, which is one of the things I like best about my grandma. If I wanted to talk to her about what I was doing, she'd be interested. If I didn't want to, that was fine, too.

I closed my book and looked out at Salt Lake City. Mostly Mormons lived here. Declan knows his history, and as we drove through the city he told us all these true stories and legends about the Mormons. Like the one about the seagulls who ate the crickets that were eating the crops of the first Mormon pioneers. It's cool stuff.

When I wasn't looking out the window or taking notes, I watched Charles Stavros. You could have been fooled into thinking he was interested, the way he kept looking right at Declan. But I noticed he never even glanced out the windows. I took out my notebook and wrote: Looks like a man with a mission. But what is his mission? As a writer you must not let a thought or a good phrase slip away. I know a lot about the techniques of writing, but could I pull it off? "Never sell yourself short," Joan Lowery Nixon had told us when she came to visit our class. "Have confidence!"

Okay, Joan.

When we stopped to see the Beehive House, Charles Stavros stayed on the bus.

"Poor man, that is such an enormous bandage on his hand," Grandma said. "I wonder if he's in pain."

"I wonder what he did to it," I said. Hmm! What, indeed?

When the bus pulled in at Temple Square in the middle of the city, Charles Stavros did "disembark," as Declan calls it. I guess that was because this was the lunch stop.

Declan held up a hand to keep us all in place while

he made an announcement. His red, white, and blue shirt dazzled in the sun that came in through the windows. "You can all leave your stuff in the bus. It will be perfectly safe. The coach will be locked and Scotty will be with it."

Almost all the passengers, including Grandma and me, left the red carry-ons behind. Cameras and binoculars bounced against chests. But one bag was taken off the bus. Charles Stavros's.

We straggled along behind Declan in pairs or small groups.

Geneva and her dad walked in front of Grandma and me, a gigantic space between them. I decided there was another mystery there, but one was enough for me to concentrate on. I think that's a rule in mystery books. You have to focus on one thing at a time.

Charles Stavros walked alone, the red bag cradled against his chest.

The group met up at the cafeteria. We had tables for eight, and by careful maneuvering I made sure Grandma and I were at Stavros's table. With us were Midge Ketchikan, the two Doves, and Millie and Beth Yokomata. Millie was a paralegal, which meant she worked for lawyers. Beth was a nurse. Millie was fat, Beth was thin. Millie talked and laughed nonstop. Beth was quiet. Millie ate lots and lots. Beth picked.

Charles Stavros ordered a turkey sandwich on wheat, a green salad, and iced tea. Ordinary. Normal. Not so normal was the way he held the bag on his lap the whole time he was eating. How odd was that? Wouldn't most people put it under the chair? He'd spread his napkin, not over his knees but over the red bag that was balanced there.

The Doves smiled happily around the table. "Isn't this pleasant?" Mrs. Dove said. Her name suited her. She was little and gray and plump. You almost wanted to stroke her.

"How many dogs do you have in your kennel?" she asked Midge.

"Twenty-eight. My husband was going to come. In the end he decided to stay with the animals. We have an assistant, but . . ."

The Doves nodded, understanding.

So Midge had a dog kennel. Twenty-eight dogs! What a racket at doggie dinnertime!

Charles Stavros poured Thousand Island dressing over his salad.

"I have a dog," he said.

I was surprised that he was getting into the conversation.

"A puppy, I should say," he went on.

"Did you board her?" Midge asked. "Or him?"

"She's a female. Yes, I boarded her, and I had a hard time saying good-bye."

"What kind is she?" Midge sounded sympathetic.

"A golden lab. Her name is Sunshine."

"She'll miss you. But she'll be fine."

I took a sip of my lemonade and thought about my story. Would a really bad guy be this nice about his puppy? Would he even have a dog? Even worse, a puppy named Sunshine?

Then I remembered that characters should not be one-dimensional and I cheered up. A bad guy who loved his dog was probably excellent to have in a book. Possible, maybe, in real life, too.

Grandma remarked on how interesting her morning had been. She had been to hear the Mormon Tabernacle Choir and told about how she had heard them singing like angels once before, the last time she was in Salt Lake City. Which, of course, had been with my grandpa all those years ago. She must be missing him a lot.

I was secretly squeezing her hand under the tablecloth when I heard Millie say to Charles Stavros, "My sister and I are from New York, too, Charles. I'm with Stevens, Smith, and Purdue, attorneys at law, on Thirty-seventh Street. My sister's a nurse at Saint Mark's."

Stavros nodded.

Then Millie leaned across the table. "You know, Charles, I could swear I've seen you before." She looked inquiringly at Beth, but Beth just raised one skinny black eyebrow and shook her head.

"I'm sure of it." Millie tapped her forehead. "It'll come. Maybe you were a murderer and Bryson Smith got you off. He's our defense attorney." She laughed and added, "Only kidding."

"I know," Stavros said, and went on eating. He was having trouble using his left hand. I deduced that he was normally right-handed and also that his injury must be recent. I'd make a note of that in my book as soon as we got back to the bus.

"Hey! I think I saw your picture in the paper," Millie exclaimed. "That's what it was. You were one of those guys they rounded up who they thought might be involved in the hijacking."

Everyone gasped.

Millie put her hand over her mouth. "Oh, shoot! No wonder my sister bought me a T-shirt that said 'God, put your arms around me and your hand over my mouth.'"

I sat up straight. What was she saying? I couldn't believe my luck. Here was the absolute start. My novel might even turn out to be true-life, nonfiction, like that Truman Capote one. Giddyup! I was on my way.

"I'm terribly sorry, Charles," Millie went on. "What an awful thing to even think. Just because you look—" She gulped. "In fact, I'm perfectly sure that's not where I saw you. I swear! Those were all suspected terrorists. Stupid words just pour out of me. I should wear that T-shirt every day of my life."

Charles Stavros didn't smile. "I'm sure you were only kidding," he said.

"She was, of course." Beth scowled at her sister.

"She didn't mean it at all." Grandma's face was a little pink.

The Doves made small cooing noises of dismay.

"Could you pass the rolls, please?" Midge asked loudly.

I took a bite of my sandwich. They were all sorry for Charles Stavros. But what if Millie was right? Suspected terrorists. I was just about positive that's exactly where she'd seen him. She worked in an attorney's office, after all. What if he really, truly was a terrorist? Wouldn't it be great if she'd cut out that picture? And had it with her? And we were able to identify him? But why would she have it with her? If I read that in a mystery book, I wouldn't believe it. If she remembered where she'd seen it, maybe I could track it on my computer when I got home.

Beth spoke into the long, embarrassed silence. "If you need your bandage changed, Charles, I could do that for you. Anytime."

Stavros looked up. "Thanks. I've arranged to have it re-dressed when we get to Wyoming. I have a friend who's a physician in Cody."

"What happened to it, anyway?" Millie asked. She'd made a quick recovery from her screwup remark and was back on target.

"I hurt it." The way Stavros said the words, it was pretty obvious he wasn't going to answer any more questions.

"Must have been hurt really bad to need a bandage that size," Millie muttered.

Her sister gave her a "shut up" look.

We were all finished eating and there was general rejoicing that Star Tours would be picking up the tab for the meal.

"If I'd known," Millie said, "I'd have had two desserts." She added again, "Only kidding."

"I'm going to the restroom," Grandma whispered to me, and I nodded.

Mr. Dove and the men from the other table were already heading toward the men's room.

"Mr. Dove, will you keep an eye on my grandson?" Grandma asked.

"Of course." Mr. Dove gave a little, old-fashioned kind of bow.

Wasn't Charles Stavros coming? I loitered a bit,

waiting, folding my napkin, taking another sip of water, keeping nice Mr. Dove waiting, too.

After a minute Stavros brushed a few crumbs from his red bag, took it in his left hand, and got up.

Mr. Dove and I were right behind him.

He took the bag with him into one of the stalls. Quickly I popped into the one next to him even though it would have been polite to let Mr. Dove go first, since all the other stall doors were closed. Safe inside, I bent down and peeked below the partition.

There was no red bag on the floor of the next stall. Stavros must still be holding it. Or maybe there was a hook and he had hung it up. There was no hook on the back of my door. I just knew there was something so important in that bag that he didn't want to let go of it, even when he was peeing.

I quickly stepped out again and stood washing my hands at the sink, listening for the door of his stall to open.

When it did, he came over to the washbasin next to mine. He set the bag on the counter between us and rested his bandaged hand protectively on top of it. I watched in the mirror as he pumped the liquid soap on his left hand, having a hard time, pushing the soap button then quickly catching the blob before it dropped into the basin.

I looked at him in the mirror. That heavy black hair, that dark skin, that mustache, those piercing eyes. Was that how Greeks looked? Or . . . ? Suppose what Millie said was true. That he was a terrorist. *What if he had a bomb in that bag and was planning on blowing up our bus?* A shiver chased along my bones. I considered the way he looked; the way he clutched that red bag, the way he kept to himself all the time, aloof from the rest of us; and Millie's memory of the photo.

Realistically, though, why would he want to blow up a tour bus? But what if the bus wasn't his target? What if it was some important building we would pass along the way? I should definitely tell someone. Grandma? Or Declan? What would I say? I needed some kind of proof. And anyway, I could be imagining all this. After all, I was a writer, or I should say, I was going to be a writer. Writers had lots of imagination, which was an asset, like in the Harry Potter books. But this wasn't just a story. This could be a true emergency.

I waited, leaning across the washbasin, using so much soap that the lather bubbled up onto my arms.

As soon as Charles Stavros's left hand was safely under the running water I turned my faucet on stronger and scooched the water that poured out of it onto the red bag, which rested between us. Unfortunately, some of it splashed on his bandage, too.

"Oh!" I gasped. "Oh, no! I'm sorry."

Mr. Dove was washing up on my other side. "No harm done, I'm sure, Kevin," he said.

"I don't know how I did that," I said, though of course I knew exactly how I'd done it. "Here's a paper towel to dry off your bandage," I said, yanking one out of the dispenser. I snatched up the bag, pulled down a bunch more paper towels, and began frantically wiping it off. "I'll do this."

The bag was heavy. It felt like there were hard, bumpy things inside. I gave it a little secret shake but nothing rattled. It had dark water splotches all over it, thanks to me.

Stavros seized the bag from me and dabbed at the water himself. "It's all right," he whispered. His voice was as tender as if he were talking to a baby. My ears felt like they were on fire. Stavros was talking either to Mr. Dove or to Geneva's dad, who had just emerged from the end stall, or to me. Or to himself. Or to someone or something in that bag. I was pretty sure it wasn't to me or to any of the others. Or to himself, either.

CHAPTER

3

The next day, day three, we got on the bus, left Salt Lake City, and drove north, along the edge of the Great Salt Lake. This lake sure is a big sucker! Declan told us that it's about eighty miles long and thirty-five miles wide and that it probably had once been part of a much larger lake, long, long ago. He said we'd stop for photographs later and there'd be a chance to swim for anyone who wanted to.

There was a chorus of "Are you kidding?" and "No way!"

The Texans began singing something about three

little fishes and Grandma said to me, "That song's as old as I am. Their grandmothers must have taught them."

We all applauded at the end, and Declan said, "Very nice! But you'll not see any little fishes in the Great Salt Lake. There are only brine shrimp."

He went on to tell us more about the lake, how it's so buoyant you couldn't sink in it even if you tried. You'd bob up like a cork. He said the water was saltier than that in any ocean in the world.

I jotted down some notes for future mystery novels (something that Mrs. Nixon strongly advises). What if someone, not knowing as much about the Great Salt Lake as I do, had murdered someone and thrown the body into the water, thinking it would sink and be gone forever, and it popped up, and kept popping up? I liked that idea a lot. But it wasn't happening here. And the key word was "focus."

I was closing the notebook when I heard two voices calling to Declan.

"*We* want to swim. Absolutely."

Buffo and Blessing Roberts.

"Are there changing rooms, Declan?" Blessing asked.

"There are. Out at the end of the causeway."

"Great!"

I turned around and saw Buffo and Blessing smiling happily at each other.

Grandma shuddered. "As I recall, that lake may be one of the natural wonders of the world but it's not very attractive for bathing. Unless it has changed."

I had no hope that Charles Stavros would go for a swim and leave his bag behind. If he did swim, it would be pretty hard for him to hold the bag over his head. And what about his bandage?

Scotty pulled the coach into the parking area and we began to file out.

Buffo and Blessing jogged ahead of the rest of us, heading for the lake. They had white towels around their necks and carried black swimsuits. In their shorts their behinds were very big but I noticed they didn't jiggle. All muscle, I thought.

Grandma and I walked behind Stavros.

Geneva and her dad were ahead of him. I couldn't help observing again the space between them and the way she kept her face turned away from him as if there was something really interesting on the other side of the lake.

Still, it surprised me when Grandma said, "That little girl is very troubled. I talked with her father at breakfast. He's an engineer and he's just back from Africa. It seems he spends a lot of time there."

I don't know why I was surprised that Grandma knew so much. People tell her things. I think it's because she's such a good listener.

"Was Geneva in Africa, too?" I asked.

"No. I don't think his wife was, either. There's a sadness about him. Have you noticed?"

I shook my head.

Charles Stavros was hugging the red bag against his chest. I noticed everything about *him*. Wouldn't a regular person carrying a regular bag sling it over his shoulder? Was there something in there he didn't want to get bumped? In case it would get broken? Or hurt? Could it possibly be his puppy—that he hadn't been able to leave it after all? But a puppy would whine or bark. And it would have to be fed. And it would need to go to the bathroom. But if he had a bomb . . . It wouldn't be good for a bomb to get bumped. I froze at the thought.

Grandma was looking at me strangely. "Are you all right, Kevin?"

I realized that I had stopped walking.

I bent over. "Something in my shoe." I untied my shoelace and shook my sneaker vigorously. "Got it," I said.

Buffo and Blessing disappeared into the dressing rooms while the rest of us gazed at the lake. We actually stood well back because the shores were thick with kelp or some sort of weed. Tiny black flies hopped and swarmed silently around it.

Millie took out a tissue and held it to her mouth as if she was afraid one of them was going to jump in.

"Nasty." Mrs. Dove gave a small ladylike shudder. "I suppose the . . . the swimmers . . . will have to go through that to get in the water?"

"No other way, my dear," Mr. Dove said.

"They must be crazy," Millie muttered. "I hope they don't bring any of those flies back in the bus with us. You know, in their hair or crawling around."

"Millie!" Beth said sharply.

31

Millie took a deep breath. "Only kidding."

We waited as Buffo and Blessing emerged from the dressing rooms in black swimsuits that were identical, except that Blessing's had a top. They each had a red tattoo on the right shoulder, but from where I stood I couldn't see what it was. Hand in hand they plunged in, making whooping noises, the flies rising around them like shifting black clouds, kelp clinging to their legs.

"Gross!" Geneva started to scratch herself all over even though the flies were nowhere near us.

We watched Buffo and Blessing lying on top of the water, their heads and toes and bellies poking up.

"It's great," they shouted. "You could sleep in here. It's a humongous water bed."

The Texans began a chorus of "Shoo, Fly, Don't Bother Me," and Midge moved closer to Grandma and whispered, "Who needs the Mormon Tabernacle Choir when we've got them, Mrs. Saunders?"

I wondered if I should ask Midge, since she was a dog expert, if a little puppy could live in a Star Tours bag and never bark, whine, or go to the bathroom. But I decided not to. It might not be a good idea to get any of the tour people involved with my mystery just yet. I'd wait and watch my suspect some more until I had proof.

There weren't too many people visiting the Great Salt Lake today. Buffo and Blessing were the only two floaters. At a distance, three people walked along the path, two dogs frolicking beside them. The dogs kept darting off to leap into the kelp, biting and snapping at the rising flies. Suddenly they seemed to see us, and they came at a gallop, tails wagging, ears turned inside out, pink tongues lolling.

"Hello, ladies," Beth said, bending to stroke one as it streaked past her.

Millie lit a cigarette and laughed. "They're gentlemen." She held out a hand but the dogs ignored her.

"Probably they don't care for the smell of tobacco," Beth said, waving smoke away from the front of her face.

One of the dogs suddenly stopped, legs rigid, then raced straight at Charles Stavros. The other followed, his nose in the air.

Stavros saw them coming and instantly lifted the red bag at arm's length over his head.

The dogs leaped, trying to reach it. They were big dogs, with shiny black coats. One of them had his paws on Stavros's chest. The dog didn't look menacing, just excited.

"Get down! Get away!" Stavros shouted.

Geneva's father rushed toward him, and so did Midge. Midge pulled on the collar, but the dog was too strong. Stavros was almost knocked off balance as he staggered back, the bag high above his head. I remembered how heavy it had been.

"Woof, woof," the dogs laughed. "Woof!"

I started forward, but Grandma grabbed my arm. "Stay right here, Kevin," she said.

From the lake Buffo shouted, "Hey! What's going on?" He and Blessing had their heads lifted to see better, and I thought how much they looked like the black otters I'd seen in Monterey Bay, lying on their backs munching on abalone.

The dogs' owners sprinted along the path, shouting, "Primo! Casper! Stop that this minute." As if on cue the dogs dropped down, shamefaced, and stood with their tails dragging.

The owners were apologizing to Stavros and clipping heavy leashes on the dogs. "Bad boys," they scolded. And then to Stavros: "They weren't going to hurt you, honest. They're really gentle."

"You could have fooled me," Millie said quite nastily.

"It's all right." Stavros yanked down on his windbreaker, which had risen almost to his armpits.

"It's whatever you have in that bag that attracted them," one of the owners, a guy with a spotty face, said. "Do you have steaks? They do go crazy for steaks." He gave a little nervous laugh.

"No. No steaks," Stavros said.

Geneva stood next to me. "What do you think he *does* have?" she asked. "It's weird how he never lets go of that bag. Everywhere he goes, it goes."

"I've noticed," I said, casually.

She stared at me. "I think you know something," she said.

I couldn't help noticing that her eyes were a much darker blue than the lake behind her. Of course, her eyes were probably not as salty. And you definitely couldn't float in them.

Buffo and Blessing came trudging out of the lake

through the kelp and flies. Their spiky red hair had turned dark in the salt water. "That was terrific," Buffo said. "A once-in-a-lifetime experience."

"Exhilarating," Blessing called out as they headed for the showers. The tattoo on her shoulder was a red heart with BUFFO printed in it. His was identical, except it said BLESSING.

"Sorry we missed all the excitement," Buffo said to Charles Stavros. "What were the hounds of the Baskervilles after, anyway?"

Charles Stavros shrugged, held the bag close against him, and headed back toward the bus.

CHAPTER

4

I decided to make Geneva my partner, or actually my assistant. Even Sherlock Holmes had Watson. And two watchers might be better than one.

As we were getting back on the bus I told her, "You said you thought I knew something about Charles Stavros. I don't. I suspect. We could discuss it if you like. I'll ask my grandma if she minds if you and I sit together for a while." I knew Grandma would say "Fine," and I was right. She believed Geneva was troubled, and she would think I might help her. "You can ask your dad if it's okay," I said.

Geneva sniffed. "I don't care if it's okay with him or not. He's left me plenty of times," she said.

We sat in one of the empty seats at the back.

"One good thing about a bus," I said. "Stavros isn't getting off until the bus stops. It's easy to keep an eye on him."

"Is that our plan? To keep an eye on him? You mean because of the bag?"

I nodded and took out my mystery notebook. "I've been writing down things about him in case we need them for evidence," I told her.

"Write about the dogs," Geneva ordered.

I gave her a cold look. "I'm going to." Maybe this wasn't going to work. It wouldn't if she turned out to be impossibly bossy. This was my mystery and she was just lucky I was sharing. "Here," I said. "You can read."

She flipped through the pages. "You don't have much," she said.

I gave her another look. "I'll get more."

"We," she said. "We'll get more."

Was she going to be a total affliction?

I leaned toward her. "I thought he might have a

bomb in there. He definitely looks like someone who could be carrying a bomb."

Geneva's eyes opened wide. "He does look exactly like a terrorist. I've never seen a real one, but I've seen pictures on TV."

"Listen to this." I told her what Millie had said about the photograph in the newspaper.

"Oh, wow!" Geneva breathed.

"I bet he's not even Greek," I went on. "But I can't figure out how he could have gotten a bomb past the security at the airport in New York. My grandma wasn't even allowed to bring her knitting needles. She had to buy new ones in Salt Lake City."

"Maybe he bought a new *bomb* in Salt Lake City," Geneva said.

I caught my breath. "Hey! He was late, remember? What if he had an accomplice who brought it to him the night before? Or that morning?"

Geneva looked smug. "That's what I was thinking. Actually, that's what I said. But wait!" She tugged at a tuft of her yellow hair. "If he has a bomb, he could blow us up anytime. Just ka-boom and we'd be all in pieces."

We stared at each other. I flashed back to the Twin Towers and 9/11, the terrible pictures with the smoke and the screaming, running people. A bomb in a bus wouldn't kill thousands, like that. But it would kill us.

"Why would he want to?" I was mad at my voice for sounding so babyish. "We're not important. Are we?"

We sat back. I half heard Declan telling us that we were now in Idaho, and how Meriwether Lewis and William Clark explored the region, after crossing the Bitterroot Range, and about the fur-trading forts and the Nez Perce Indians. It was probably great stuff and the kind of thing my parents wanted me to learn about on this trip, but I had immediate, pressing problems to deal with, not ancient history.

I was glad when he started on one of his long, dumb jokes—about an old prospector—and I could turn him all the way off. What if I went up to him right now and confided my suspicions? After all, he'd be smarter than Geneva. But I was back to the same old thing. All I had were suspicions, and as Geneva had so rudely pointed out, I didn't have much to base them on.

I was thinking hard. "*We're* not important. But suppose one of the other passengers is? Suppose one of them is a . . . a senator or a . . . a general in the United States Army . . . or the vice president of the United States in disguise?"

Geneva looked thoughtful. "Maybe."

We reeled off the names of the people in the tour group. "The Doves?" I said. "Impossible. Buffo and Blessing—the two otters? Couldn't be. Millie and Beth?"

"If Millie were the vice president of the United States, she'd have blabbed about it already," Geneva said.

"Besides," I added, "she doesn't trust Stavros, either. Midge? I can't imagine her being a general in the army."

Geneva bristled. "Why? Because she's a woman?"

"No. Because she looks after dogs. She doesn't have time to do army stuff. Could be one of the Texans. Who from Texas would be so important on this trip that a terrorist would want to blow *that person* up?"

Geneva shook her head. "I can't think of anyone."

We sat staring at the seat-back in front of us, hoping for inspiration.

"Your grandma, then," Geneva said at last.

"My grandma! Get serious! What about your dad?"

"He's too busy working for the Africans. He's too busy even for us."

Uh-oh, I thought. Better to stay off the subject of her dad.

Geneva sighed. "We're stymied."

I stood up, pretending to stretch, grabbing a look at Charles Stavros. I couldn't see the red bag but I knew it was there, right next to him.

"Still aboard?" Geneva asked.

I thought she was probably being sarcastic, so I sarcasted right back. "No, he jumped out the window but we didn't notice."

Geneva giggled.

I hoped she was taking this seriously. "This is not a game, you know," I said.

She sniffed in an offended way and said, "Not to me."

Then I told her my last idea.

"I think it's a building he's after," I said. "A building

we stop at. Or pass."

"What building?"

I shrugged. "How do I know?"

We crossed the border from Idaho into Wyoming, the forty-fourth state admitted to the Union. Declan told us how the pioneers had streamed west on the California, Mormon, and Oregon Trails. He told us about the great blizzard of 1887, in which thousands of cattle died. When he said part of Wyoming had once belonged to Texas, there was a cheer from the four Texans. I was afraid they might burst into song, but they didn't. I guessed they were miffed that Texas had ever had to give up anything.

Geneva and I were quiet, inspiration gone.

I gazed out of the window at the endless grass-lands, the rivers, the cattle grazing peacefully. It was good to give my brain a rest. I let myself imagine how it must have been, back in the days of Jim Bridger, the famous trapper and mountain man, the days of the covered wagons, creaking along the narrow trails. Bison would have been everywhere. It must have been beautiful. And it was beautiful still.

We stopped in the town of Jackson outside a big, old-time-looking wooden hotel with a porch all the way around it.

"I bet Jim Bridger tied his horse up to one of those posts," Geneva said.

"Yep." I could just see it.

"One hour," Declan announced. "Scotty will pick us up again right where he lets us off. You're welcome to sit awhile on the porch and have yourselves a cold drink. Or wander the town, if you like."

"On guard," Geneva whispered, sliding out of her seat.

She and I were the last off the bus. I immediately checked for Charles Stavros. There he was, standing aloof from everyone, red bag securely against his chest.

"Check your watches," Declan said. "We'll get under way at four sharp. We want to make it to Grand Teton National Park in time for our elegant dinner at Jackson Lake Lodge."

Millie and Beth were standing right next to us.

"You know what?" Millie said to me. "I'm dying to know what Stavros has in that bag. I might just ask him. It's always better to be straightforward."

Beth groaned. "Give us a break, Millie. You don't mean straightforward. You mean nosy."

Geneva nudged me and we made sure we were close by as Millie wandered casually up to Stavros.

"I'm leaving," Beth said. "You are such an embarrassment sometimes, Mill."

"Go for it, Millie," Geneva breathed.

Millie gave Stavros a bogus smile. "Hi, Chuck. Do you like to be called Chuck? It's friendly, don't you think?"

"Actually, it may be friendly but I don't like it." His smile under his mustache was just as bogus as hers.

Geneva gave an excited little hiss.

Millie leaned forward and touched the red bag with the tip of her finger. "Your bag must have something very valuable in it. I mean, even those two black dogs, Primo and whatever his name was, wanted to know."

Stavros took a step back. For a second I thought he was going to hold the bag above his head the way he did with the dogs. He stood before her like a mountain, maybe as big as one of the Tetons we were going to see later. "It is valuable to me, yes," he said. "Now, if you'll excuse me." He stepped toward her and this time Millie was the one who moved back.

"Well, what an ignoramus," she muttered as he walked away. Her face was red and mottled, like a chicken's comb. "You just wait, Mr. so-called Charles Stavros." She turned to me. "I've called my friend Paulie back at the office. He's going to get that picture from the *Times* and fax it to me tomorrow at the Old Faithful Inn in Yellowstone. We'll be there day after next. Then we shall see what we shall see, and find out just who Stavros is."

"Will you show the picture to us?" Geneva asked.

"Show it to you? I'll show it to the police, that's what I'll do."

She whirled away.

"Ooh, she's mad!" Geneva said. "Just imagine, though, if she's right."

Midge had been leaning against the porch railing. "I overheard a bit of that," she said mildly. "I just want to say that if Mr. Stavros's puppy lay against that bag, back in his apartment, or if she maybe urinated on it, the bag would be a big attraction to dogs.

Especially to male dogs."

Geneva held her nose. "Gross," she muttered.

I wanted to have a tantrum, right there. Were all my mysterious clues going to turn out to have ordinary explanations? No, there was still the question of what was in that bag.

Geneva's dad came up then and said: "Geneva. Would you like to take a walk up Main Street?"

"Sorry, Kevin and I are going to the Cowboy Emporium," Geneva said.

It was the first I'd heard of it.

"Oh," her father said. Just that one word before he turned away.

"Why are you so mean to him?" I asked.

Geneva tossed her head, which would have been a lot more dramatic if she'd had long hair instead of those yellow clumps. "Want to go to the emporium?"

"Sure. Just let me check with Grandma," I said.

Grandma said okay. But she told us to stay together and not be too long.

The Cowboy Emporium was just across the street. There was a statue of a cowboy on his horse at the doorway and an Indian war bonnet in the window, and I did want to go in.

I looked along Main Street. No cowboys in sight. No Indians in war bonnets or feathers. No covered wagons. Just traffic, plenty of it. SUVs and trucks, and even a Hummer. There were women in shorts and skimpy tops; young guys with skateboards; a teenager with dyed blond hair, a nose ring, and a USC sweatshirt. I figured Jackson wasn't the way it used to be. Jim Bridger would never have recognized it.

And then . . . and then I saw something that gave me such a great idea my head almost burst open. Sometimes good ideas just jump into my brain.

"Not the emporium," I said. "I want to go to that bookstore farther along."

"For what? Another one of that author's mystery books?"

"Not this time. Come on."

The Step Inside Bookshop had paperbacks for sale in bins on the sidewalk. A black cat slept in the window. There was a poster for a new Harry Potter novel.

We stepped inside and a bell rang. Immediately there was that great bookstore smell. I'm not sure if reading has a smell, but that's what I always think of when I'm around books. It's the smell of secrets hidden, and words and thoughts. And adventures.

"I could stay in here all day," I muttered.

"We only have a half hour left, so hurry up. I still want to go to that emporium."

It was the kind of bookstore I love, where nobody bothers you. You can just browse.

I walked along the aisles, not allowing myself to stop and look till I came to the travel section. My fingers trailed along the spines. What if the Step Inside didn't have what I wanted? But, great! There it was! An English-Greek, Greek-English dictionary.

"Eureka!" I said, which might even be a Greek word, for all I know. It means "I've got it!"

Geneva beamed, I think admiringly. "Now I see what you're planning," she said. "You're going to say something to him in Greek and see if he answers."

I nodded. "Right."

The dictionary cost $12.95, which was a lot for a book I didn't actually intend to read. Expensive, but worth it.

Outside again, I checked down the street. Stavros

was sitting upright in a chair on the wooden porch, all by himself, the bag on his knees.

Grandma and some of the other tour members plus two old fellows in overalls and cowboy hats were clustered around a big table, drinking what—from where I stood—looked like iced tea. I realized I was superthirsty.

I opened the bookstore bag and took out the dictionary.

"Don't look at it now," Geneva said in an impatient voice. "We won't have time to stop at the emporium."

"So?" I stopped and opened it. "Let's talk to Mr. Stavros," I said. "Let's find out if that Greek man understands Greek."

"**H**urry!" Geneva urged. "If we're going to see any-thing in the emporium, we have to bounce!"

"You go." I went back to thumbing through the dictionary. I didn't even watch her huff away.

The beginning of the dictionary was English-Greek. What would I say to him? I'd say, "Have a nice day." That was ordinary. No. I needed some-thing he would have to answer. How about . . . ? I flipped through the pages, which were like tissue paper. The kind where you have to lick your fingers if the school librarian isn't watching. The print was small. I'd look for the word "what."

WHAT. . . τι

Oh, no! I rapidly looked down the page. All the Greek words were spelled with funny characters that didn't even look like letters. Here was "you": εσύ.

How on earth was I supposed to pronounce that? I saw a low wall outside a pharmacy and I sat on it and finger-licked all the way through the English-Greek.

Surely somewhere there would be a pronunciation guide. Phonetic. What use was it if there wasn't a single word that I could decipher or even begin to say? How could "do" be spelled έχω? What kind of a stupid dictionary didn't even tell you how to say the words? I felt like throwing it down and giving it a good, hard kick.

Well, my plan wasn't going to work. A good idea gone bad. My mom has a saying, something about best-laid plans often go awry, which means they get messed up when you're not looking, and she was sure right.

Someone was calling my name. My grandma. The tour group had gathered on the porch and our big bus was stopping in front of the hotel. Charles Stavros waited behind the others.

I didn't even have time to take the useless book back and get my $12.95. That stunk.

Geneva came careening out of the Cowboy Emporium doors wearing a bright blue cap that said CODY RODEO QUEEN on the front. "I'm going to be ready when we get to Cody," she said, beaming happily. Her yellow hair stuck out at the back like chicken feathers.

We waited for a traffic break to cross the street. "How's the book?" she asked. "What are you going to do next?"

"I'm awry," I told her.

"What?"

"I'm so blown away about the book—" I began.

Wait a second! In a mystery novel there are always obstacles for the hero to overcome. Which he always does by thinking hard and fiercely and coming up with a plan. In fact, obstacles are good in a book; they show the hero's spunk and brains. I thought hard and fiercely, then swung around to face Geneva.

"I've got a plan."

"Again?"

"Yeah."

"Hope you enjoyed your short visit in Jackson," Declan was saying.

"C'mom, c'mon, tell me the plan," Geneva urged.

"Shh! I'm not ready yet to divulge," I told her.

"We're on our way now to Grand Teton National Park," Declan announced. "Can you find it on your map?"

He held his up to display. "The Tetons rise almost a mile above Jackson. We'll see all kinds of wildlife here. Keep your eyes open. You might see black bears or mountain lions. The black bear cubs are usually born in the middle of winter, but by now we could see them foraging for themselves."

"So, are you ready to divulge now?" Geneva asked. Geneva can have a sarcastic way of saying things that is very off-putting.

"Not yet," I said coldly, and she began looking out the window and humming in a very irritating manner.

I noticed that Midge had moved across to sit next to Grandma and that Geneva's dad was reading a paperback titled *The Boer War*, by Winston Churchill.

"Does your dad read a lot?" I asked Geneva.

She shrugged. "How would I know?"

I hesitated. "Don't you ever talk to him?"

She turned her navy blue stare on me. "I say please and thank you."

Back to my plan. Would Stavros answer a question in Greek? Would he blow his cover? I tried to concentrate, which was hard because of the humming and because every few minutes Declan would get superexcited and shout, "Moose! Moose to the left!" and everyone would crowd around the windows on the left to see the huge animals grazing just a few feet from the road. The moose would raise their big heads to stare at us as we passed. It wasn't hard to see we were more interested in them than they were in us. Or Declan would call, "Elk! Elk to the right!" and there they'd be, so elegant, stepping through the long grass. Cameras clicked and flashed.

Twice we stopped for better photo opportunities. Once we crossed a field covered with thistles and weeds and humongous pancakes of moose dung to get a close-up of a moose calf standing, big-eyed, next to its mother.

I was afraid all these interruptions would make me lose my focus.

Both times we got off the bus, Charles Stavros took his red bag.

Both times, I checked that he got back on and that he had the bag with him. Then, for the first time, I saw Stavros interested in something other than his bag.

He was sitting with his head bent over the map, studying it intently. He had taken out a pencil and was making marks on the map. A shiver chased up my backbone and my ears tingled. Was he looking for the town, or the place, or the building he wanted to bomb? The monument? Could there possibly be a secret nuclear test site out here? I pulled out the map, unfolded it, and ran my finger along the route we would take. I think it had been specially printed for Star Tours; it showed all the places we'd stop and the scenic routes we'd travel to get there. Yellowstone; Old Faithful; Cody, where we'd be going to the rodeo; Mount Rushmore.

When I looked again at Stavros he'd folded the map and poked it into the mesh pocket in front of him.

Somewhere on the bus a phone rang.

I craned my neck to look ahead. Millie was talking into her cell, nodding her head. I saw her slide the phone into her red carry-on. Even from where we sat, she seemed pleased. She looked around, then stood and came to talk to us.

"That's that!" she said. Her face was pink, not red and angry the way it had been when she talked to Charles Stavros in Jackson. "The *Times* picture is waiting for us at the Old Faithful Inn." Her voice purred with satisfaction. "I'm almost sure I'm right about . . ." She twitched her head toward Charles Stavros's seat. "I wish now I'd told Paulie to send the clipping to the Jackson Lake Lodge instead. I can't wait for the confrontation."

"She's not 'only kidding,' either," Geneva whispered as Millie swayed her way back to her seat. "She can't wait. But you don't think she would actually confront him, do you? I mean, if he is what we think he is, that could be really dangerous."

"I think she'll show us first. We'll vote for going to the cops."

"Or not," Geneva said. "If he turns out to be okay."

"Meantime . . . ," I said, and I began to carefully tear a page from my mystery notebook. I hate tearing pages out of notebooks. It defaces them. "Deface" is a very good word and means "to spoil the appearance of." As in, "Boys! You must not deface the walls in the boys' bathroom."

I opened the English-Greek dictionary and spread it across my knees.

Geneva peered at the open dictionary pages. "Are you starting now on the famous plan?" she asked. "Ack! I see what you mean about the words. How does anyone talk this stuff?"

"I guess it's easy if you're Greek," I said.

"Well, what are you going to do?"

It wasn't easy to write this stuff, either. If you weren't Greek.

Carefully I copied the word for "Dear" onto the

torn-out notebook page, then added, "Mr. Stavros."

"Are you going to tell me what you're doing?" Geneva asked.

I was remembering advice from my how-to-write-a-mystery book.

One of the rules: "In a mystery, the protagonist is seeking the truth, trying to find it, directly or indirectly. This is his job."

This was my job.

I began searching, searching for words, copying them carefully. There were all kinds of squiggles, which I knew must be important.

"You're writing him a *letter*? That's your plan? That's nuts!" Geneva took off her rodeo cap and scratched her head. "This itches me," she complained.

The letter was short: "Dear Mr. Stavros. What is in the bag?"

Geneva leaned across me. "Okay, what does it say?"

I translated.

She thumped her fists on her knees. "Bingo," she

whispered. "That is *so* bingo! And so not nuts."

I searched again for a new word and added "Sincerely" and my name.

"If he can read it, then he's Greek, no question," I said. "And he'll either be mad at me, or—"

Geneva interrupted. "Or answer. If he's innocent. Maybe he'll say: 'I didn't want to tell anybody, but you remember how I confessed that I hated to leave my puppy. She's here. In the bag.' And she'll be—"

"I don't think so," I said.

But right then I knew something. I didn't want him to be able to read it. I didn't want him to be Greek. I didn't want him to be innocent. I didn't want to lose my big mystery adventure. But just think how scary it would be if he wasn't Greek. If he was something else! Having a mystery also meant having a terrorist aboard. And a bomb. Criminy! What *did* I want?

I folded the paper, wrote "Charles Stavros" across it, and slipped it in the bookstore bag with my dictionary. "I'm glad I didn't take the dictionary back," I told Geneva. "It was really useful after all."

"When are you going to give him the letter?"

"At dinner," I said, and I felt my legs begin to tremble. What had Geneva said about the dangers of confronting Stavros? Maybe I shouldn't give it to him at all. Maybe this was *too* direct.

We were pulling up in front of the big Jackson Lake Lodge.

"Okay, everyone. Don't worry about your luggage," Declan called. "It will be brought to your rooms. And I have your keys right here." He jangled them above his head.

I craned forward. Stavros's room was 145.

As usual, Geneva and I were the last off. It was slow moving as people picked up their keys from Declan and checked the labels and asked all kinds of questions, like how formally they should dress tonight and if their rooms had a view of the lake. I slid the map into the bag with the dictionary and the letter. I'd work on it some more in my room.

As we inched forward, I was standing next to the seat where Charles Stavros had sat. What if he'd left the red bag behind and I could look in it myself?

Not a chance! I stood biting my lips. The only

61

thing he'd left was the map in the mesh pocket. My heart pounded.

Was anyone watching?

No.

Quick as a flick I leaned forward and slid his map out of the pocket by the two top corners.

At the very least, if the cops needed his fingerprints, now I had them!

CHAPTER

6

Grandma and I had adjoining rooms on the ground floor. My window looked out on Jackson Lake and the Grand Tetons behind it. The mountains were so awesome that I got this little catch in my throat that seems to happen when I see something beautiful. I get the same feeling when there's a great California sunset, the sun dipping red into Santa Monica Bay. Things like that.

But I had no time to stand here admiring.

I unfolded Stavros's map.

Nothing.

I took it over to the bedside table, switched on the lamp, and held the map directly beneath it.

Nothing.

But wait! I moved the map back and forth. There were some grooves that might have come from a pencil point, and when I looked closer I saw three small black crumbs. I closed my eyes and imagined Stavros writing, erasing, brushing the rubber crumbs away with the side of his hand. I'd done that myself a gazillion times. What had he written and then erased? If only I had a magnifying glass! But even then I might not be able— Suddenly my heart jumped with excitement. There was a detective trick I'd read about. If it would just work in real life the way it did in that book!

I spread the map flat under the light, fished a pencil from the bottom of my bag, and began to rub the lead point lightly over the grooves. As if by magic a wide circle came up that took in just about all the places we were going to visit on the rest of our trip. Inside its boundaries were Yellowstone, Cody, Mount Rushmore, Rapid City. Now my heart was galloping like a runaway horse. Was he going to explode the bomb somewhere inside that circle? I was almost sure that's what it meant. Why would he bother to erase it so completely if it was innocent?

I crouched over the bedside table till my legs cramped, then I hobbled to the bathroom and slapped cold water on my face. *What should I do?*

My phone rang. It was Grandma telling me she was just about to call Mom and Dad and I should come talk to them, too. So normal. So ordinary. *Should I tell her?*

Before I went to her room, I erased my pencil marks and I put the map in my mystery notebook. I'd have to be first on to the bus in the morning and put it back before Stavros missed it. I wouldn't even try to hold on to it for his fingerprints. That would be way too dangerous.

I took out the letter I'd written in Greek and reread it, knowing what it said even though I couldn't understand a single word. This letter could lead to a denouement, which is mystery-writer talk and means the solution of the plot. I hoped!

In Grandma's room we sat on the bed while she called on her cell phone.

First she talked. "We are having the most glorious

time," she told Mom. "I feel at peace here. I'm happy."

It was my turn to talk.

I told Mom I was happy, too. I told about how incredible the Tetons were. I did not mention Charles Stavros. I'd decided I would not mention my suspicions to Grandma. She should be at peace and happy. That's why we'd come on this trip. I wouldn't tell her. Not yet, anyway.

After we hung up, she and I dressed for dinner. Grandma looked nice in some sort of loose pants and a white shirt, with her necklace that has the big blue stone hanging from it, the stone that's the color of peacock feathers. I wore my one good sweater with my jeans and Grandma looked me over and told me how handsome I was. She kissed my cheek.

"Did you stay here with Grandpa?" I asked her.

She nodded and I looked to see if she was sad, but she was smiling. I guess good memories stay good. I wanted *this* trip to stay good for her, too.

I'd put the Greek letter in the bookstore bag, which felt hot in my hand. It felt so hot, I wouldn't have been surprised if it had gone up in flames.

Grandma glanced at it once but didn't ask questions.

We went up the wide staircase and she took my arm the way ladies do in old movies. At the top of the stairs was a big wide lobby with chairs and couches, but the best thing was the wall of windows that faced us, putting the mountains in a frame. I got that choky feeling again. I think Grandma gets it, too, because we both stood there, not speaking, just looking. Unfortunately, I couldn't keep my mind from slithering back to the map. To that circle. Of course, I couldn't be certain-sure that some-where inside the circle was Stavros's bomb target. Not certain-sure.

In the dining room we were led to a table for two by the window. The elegant waiter pulled out Grandma's chair for her and mine for me. He flour-ished my napkin onto my knees. I bet we had the table with the best view in the whole room.

I slipped the bookstore bag under my chair and went over my plan again, what I would do and say. If Stavros could read the question I'd written in Greek, I'd smile a bogus smile. "It's just that we've all been curious," I'd say. If he couldn't, well then . . . My thoughts went no further. *What's in the bag?*

I glanced around, but I didn't see him and immediately I panicked. The thing is, now when he was out of my sight I wondered what he was doing and my thoughts got scary. But then he came in, wearing his windbreaker and jeans and a white shirt with a tie. He walked over to an empty table for four, carrying the red bag, of course.

It was Grandma who said, "Should we move and sit with Mr. Stavros?" She refolded the napkin the waiter had spread so tenderly across her lap.

It would be a good chance to give him the letter, but I hadn't planned on having Grandma there when I did.

"We'd lose our nice view," I said.

"That's not so important," Grandma said. "I think maybe he feels awkward. You know, it's a bad time to look the way he looks, even if he's Greek and not a Saudi or an Iraqi. I don't see any of us making an effort to be friendly." She glanced at me. "I suppose you're too young to remember a song called 'Suspicious Minds'? Elvis Presley sang it."

"Never heard of it." I paused. "The thing is," I

said, "Stavros doesn't make much effort, either." I leaned over and took the bookstore bag from under my chair. "But I've written him a letter. In Greek."

"Kevin!" Grandma beamed at me. "So that's what you've been carrying! That is so *nice* of you, Kev. What did you say? How did you do it in *Greek*?" We were already walking toward his table, so I didn't have to answer, thank goodness. I felt so guilty I could hardly stand it.

Stavros stood, still holding his red carry-on, as we came over.

"May we join you?" Grandma asked.

"Certainly." He waved his bandaged hand toward the empty seats, then came behind Grandma and pulled out her chair for her.

I felt jittery.

Millie, who was two tables away, was staring at me as if Grandma and I were terrorists ourselves just because we were sitting with him.

Geneva and her dad, sharing a table with the Doves, were already eating their salads. I lifted the bookstore bag so that Geneva could see it. She slumped in her chair, as if the whole thing was too much for her, and then went on eating. Forget her! She'd be sorry she wasn't interested when I told her about the mysterious circle on Stavros's map.

While I studied the menu I watched Charles Stavros over its edge. When should I give him the letter? Now? Or after?

I decided on now and slid the letter from the bag.

My ears had started to tingle, telling me I was heading into danger.

"For me?" Stavros asked, taking the letter.

I nodded.

"Kevin wrote it in Greek for you," Grandma said, in the softest voice.

"In Greek?" He had to take his hand from the bag on his lap to open the page. I think he must have stared at it for a full minute.

I couldn't breathe. My hand shook as I lifted my glass of ice water and took a sip.

Stavros was looking at me intently across the table. "I'm afraid you'll have to translate for me. I don't speak or read Greek."

"You don't?" The words came out of me in a whoosh, and thoughts tumbled frantically in my head.

He wasn't Greek. *I knew it!* He wasn't who he was supposed to be. I was sitting next to a terrorist!

"You must have spent a lot of time writing this to me," Stavros said seriously. "May I keep it?"

"Sure," I muttered.

He folded the paper in four.

"It's too bad that you can't read it," Grandma said. She looked from his face to mine. "I guess Kevin thought he was giving you a treat."

"Yes. I'm sorry. Did you use a dictionary, Kevin?"

"Yes. I . . . I bought one."

Was there something in the way he was looking at me, something suspicious, as if he knew I had another motive and was trying to decide what it was? Tingle, tingle, tingle. I secretly massaged my left ear.

"Do you want to just tell me what it says?" he asked, then paused. "That wouldn't be much fun, though, would it? Why don't you lend me the dictionary and I'll try to work it out. It will be a sort of puzzle."

Grandma smiled. "That's a great idea. If you wouldn't mind, Mr. Stavros."

"Not a bit. It will be entertaining for me."

I took another sip of water. "Cool," I muttered. So the showdown had been postponed. What would he do when he read the question? But now—oh my gosh—he was unzipping the carry-on, right there, on his lap, across the table from me. He was going to put my letter in there next to . . . to whatever. I wanted to stand up and get a good look, but there was no way to do that. I sat tall, half leaning across the table. He had only pulled the zipper across about six inches, enough to slide the letter inside. I got a quick glimpse of something in there, something big and bulky and black, with a long, stringy black cord. And then the zipper closed again. I dropped back into my chair and managed to knock my fork to the floor. It landed with a soft, carpeted thud.

What had I seen? I had no idea. Were bombs that big anymore? Weren't they small and electronic now? Maybe it had to be a big bomb for a big explosion.

Our waiter came then with our menus and a clean fork for me. And I hadn't even asked for one. I tried to calm down as I studied the menu.

"You're not really having a hamburger, are you,

Kevin?" Grandma asked. "There's lobster and salmon and—"

"I like hamburgers." I sat back in my chair and brought the picture of what I'd seen in the bag back into focus. What was big and black and shiny? It had been shiny, hadn't it?

The waiter had taken our orders, and now Grandma was talking to Charles Stavros. "So you don't speak Greek, Mr. Stavros?"

"No. My parents brought me here from Athens when I was only two."

"That's why you don't have an accent," Grandma said.

"Right. My mother was American, from Illinois. She'd met my father on a trip with some school friends. My father . . ." He paused, lifted his hand for a second from the bag, and rubbed his bandage. "My father loved this country. My sister and I were true Americans from the start." He smiled, and his teeth flashed under his mustache. "The only Greek we ever spoke was 'baklava' or 'hummus.'"

"Both delicious," Grandma said.

73

Was all this true? Our meal arrived, and I carefully picked the raw onion out of my hamburger. I was wondering what to do next. If only I could get that red bag of his! But how?

"You'll let me borrow your Greek dictionary tomorrow, Kevin?" Stavros asked.

My insides quivered. "Sure."

"Maybe I'll learn how to speak my own native language before this trip is over," he said.

Saudi? I thought. Iraqi?

He stood again as we said good night.

"Sleep well," Grandma said.

On the way back to our rooms, she and I stopped in the gift shop and I bought a glass globe with a snow scene inside for my mom. I knew she'd love it.

Later, sitting on my bed, I studied the map again. My head was buzzing with so many questions I thought I'd never get to sleep. I got into bed at last, spread my blankey square over my pillow, and buried my face in it. It smelled of the apples I eat in bed every night at home, and of the shampoo my mom makes me use because it's organic and won't hurt the hair follicles or something. It smelled of home, and for a minute I lay there feeling lonely and scared even though Grandma was right in the next room.

I stared at the ceiling and the big-bladed ceiling fan that was slowly turning and turning. Suddenly a thought came that was so awful I sat straight up. *What was Charles Stavros doing right this minute?* Geneva and I could watch him pretty well all day, but what about the nights? And wouldn't a terrorist prefer to be active at night? The Tetons weren't enclosed in his map circle, but still. We had to watch him, just in case. I couldn't sit outside his door from now till morning, though. That was ridiculous. And even if I did that tonight, I couldn't do it every night. There were seven nights left, including tonight. I'd die of sleep deprivation. Maybe Geneva could help? She wouldn't. She'd ask if I was seriously crazy and stare at me with those navy blue eyes. No use depending on her. I knew that. So what could I do?

I switched on the lamp again and studied my how-to-write-a-mystery book. I get a lot of help from this book. One of the paragraphs said, "If you come to an impasse"—which I knew means something that you don't know how to handle—"ask yourself, 'If this were real, what would my hero do next?' He must use his ingenuity."

I laid the open book on my chest and closed my eyes. Okay. This *was* real and I was the hero, living out this mystery that, when I came to write it, would be superbelievable. "Write what you know," the book said. I definitely knew this.

Room 145 was three rooms down the corridor from mine.

I got up, wedged my door open just an inch with a wadded-up washcloth from my bathroom so I could easily get back in, and tiptoed out into the hall. It was empty and almost silent, all the doors closed. At the very end, where the elevators were, an ice machine hummed faintly. I counted along with my eyes.

Room 145. His room.

Still nobody watching.

A good detective has to be either a very quick thinker or a guy who thinks ahead. I went back into my room, got the plastic ice bucket, and took it with me. If someone saw me, if *he* saw me, I'd pretend I was going for ice, couldn't sleep, needed a cold drink of water. I walked along the corridor.

Room 145.

Nobody looking.

I put my ear to his door. Inside, a TV played.

Ah. He was probably in bed, watching a program. That sounded safe. Unless he was already out and he'd left the TV on to fool anybody watching him. That was a scary thought. Or suppose he came out later, and I wouldn't know?

But then I remembered something. It might have been from one of Mrs. Nixon's books. Reading mystery books is definitely a big help when you get yourself in a jam. Case in point: a map with a circle on it. I went quickly back to my room, tore a corner off the paper napkin that had been under the ice bucket, came back out, tiptoed again up to room 145, and wedged the small piece of paper between the door and the doorjamb. I'd get up early and check if it was still there. Then I'd know if he'd been out. If he had, I wouldn't know where—maybe it would just have been for ice. But this was the best my ingenuity could come up with. The TV was still playing softly inside his room.

I hurried back to bed, set my alarm for 5:30, and lay facedown on my blankey square again, breathing in the smell of it, letting my pulse slow down. I decided I was glad that in the future I was only going to write about mysteries, not be right smack in the middle of one.

The day after tomorrow we'd be in Yellowstone and Millie would get the newspaper picture of the suspected terrorists. Yellowstone, which was in Stavros's circle.

Tomorrow I'd have to lend him the Greek dictionary. It wouldn't take him long to translate the words I'd written.

And then what?

CHAPTER

7

I'd checked at 5:30 A.M. The paper scrap was still in the door. It was still there when Grandma and I went past on the way to breakfast at 8:00. Stavros had been safe in his room all night long.

He came into the dining room while we were eating our scrambled eggs and bacon. Grandma and I had a table for four and the nice Doves had asked if they could join us. They loved their room and the view and the whole tour but they were worried about our schedule for today.

"I'm not sure if we feel up to going on the raft

trip," Mrs. Dove told Grandma.

"We don't party like we used to," Mr. Dove added.

Grandma and I laughed.

"I think you'd like the river trip," Grandma said. "I did it when I was here with my dear Jim. My late husband," she explained. "It's perfectly comfortable and perfectly safe. You should come."

But even as I was listening I was watching Charles Stavros. His napkin covered the red bag on his knees. He was drinking coffee, his bandaged hand on the bag, the cup held awkwardly in his left hand. Now and again he lifted the napkin to gently pat his thick mustache. He saw me looking at him and gave a small nod.

I nodded, small-ly, back.

"You didn't bring the dictionary for Mr. Stavros?" Grandma asked.

"No. I didn't think he'd want to read it on the raft, going down the Snake," I said. Last night I'd remembered about today's raft trip and felt immediate relief. I could postpone his reading the letter for a little longer. Which was a cowardly thought, but one that came to me nevertheless. It was important that he read my question. But maybe not today.

Declan came by, table to table. "We'll drive to the Snake River," he said. "Bus outside in a half hour."

I was first on. By the time Stavros came aboard, his map was safely back in its place.

Scotty parked close to the river.

"Everyone!" Declan called. "Please leave your bags and cameras and other paraphernalia on the bus. Scotty will be here. I'd prefer it if you didn't take anything with you on the raft. Safety precautions."

"Should we take our jackets?" one of the Texans asked.

"I don't think you'll be cold. Maybe wet. But a jacket is okay."

As we lined up to get on the raft, I managed to stand next to Geneva and nudge her away from the others. I filled her in about the map and the circle, which I called "the Big C." I told her about how Stavros couldn't read my letter, which meant he wasn't Greek even though he'd tried to bluff it with all that talk about baklava and hummus. About how

I'd kept watch on him last night. About my clever paper-in-the-door plan.

Geneva gave a little whistle and rocked back and forth with her hands in her jeans pockets. She pulled her Cody Rodeo Queen cap down so it almost hid her eyes.

"So, he can't understand Greek and he's mapping out the best place to put the bomb." I hated the way she drawled it out, like some old-time movie villain. If she'd had a waxed mustache, she'd have been twirling the ends. Not a single compliment about my paper-in-the-door routine. Or my no-sleep night.

The line was moving and we had to join it. "There's more," I told her quickly. "But look, since I had to watch him last night, do you want to help me tonight? Take a turn?"

"Get real!" she muttered.

"Why am I not surprised?" I said. This girl wanted the excitement but none of the work. If I were paying her I'd fire her, right now.

Then I heard Declan arguing with Charles Stavros.

Geneva grabbed my arm. "Listen," she hissed.

"I'm really sorry, Charles," Declan was saying. "Maybe you didn't hear. I'd prefer that you don't take your bag on to the raft." As usual, Stavros was clutching it.

"I have to take it," he said, and he turned away, putting an end to the discussion.

"Mr. Stavros. Really," Declan called after him, then spread his hands in an "I give up" gesture.

I hurried so I was directly behind Charles Stavros as we got into the raft, even though I knew it might be dangerous. He was whispering something, not to me, not back to Declan. The words were to himself, or to the bag. "I will never let you go again," he said.

Never let what go? Who go?

What was in that bag?

I felt jumpy. But not for long. The raft trip was too good. I decided it ranked right up there as a life experience along with a dogsled ride I'd had once up on Mammoth Mountain in California and I wasn't going to waste it, Greek or no Greek. But still, I checked on Stavros and his bag every few minutes.

Not that he was going to *jump*! Keeping watch on him was getting to be a habit.

I suppose we weren't actually on a raft; it was more like a big rubber boat with high sides. Also, we all wore orange life jackets. I guess Star Tours didn't want to lose any of their group in the raging waters. Actually, the waters didn't rage that much. I loved it, though, the trees and brush on either side, the mountains with their little sprinkles of snow on top, the dark mysterious river flowing by. This was a kind of space, like recess between classes. I felt we were safe while we were on this raft. I closed my eyes and was Huckleberry Finn until Geneva leaned forward and poked me and whispered, "I have an idea how to get ahold of his bag."

I glanced again at Stavros sitting in front of me. "You mean now?"

"Uh-uh. Later."

She had such a satisfied smirk that I wanted to push her overboard. One good shove. But still, if she really had a clever idea, it would be a waste to lose it.

Declan wore a canary-yellow shirt with Indian arrowheads. He and a fellow he introduced as Lars poled us slowly along the river. Declan told us about how the Snake had changed course many, many times and left the small islands that dotted the water. He said the sagebrush had been there for thousands of years. I thought about how great, lumbering mastodons could have plodded along these banks. Saber-toothed tigers might have crouched in the mud to drink. I watched ducks gliding importantly along on the water. A bald eagle sailed across the sky, taking my breath with it, and for those few moments I almost forgot about Charles Stavros. I didn't forget that Geneva had come up with a plan to get his red bag. Some dopey scheme, probably. I shook my head. Forget them both!

"I'm so glad you brought me along on this trip," I whispered to Grandma.

"I'm so glad you're with me," she whispered back.

"Aren't we going to get any whitewater?" Buffo asked. "No rapids? No whirlpools? This is too tame."

"Not this trip," Declan said. "But at least nobody's getting seasick."

The Texans sang "Michael, Row the Boat Ashore" and it sounded just right, just perfect.

"Did you know that the four of them are in a choral group in Houston?" Grandma asked. "They're really excellent."

That made me smile. It was pretty nice, how the tour people told Grandma everything!

In the bus, on the return ride to the lodge, Geneva gave me the sign to come sit in back with her.

"Geneva wants to talk to me," I told Grandma, and she said, "Go on back, sweetie. I'm perfectly happy sitting here, drinking in the scenery and rejoicing. Look at those clouds! Did you ever see such a sky?"

I admired the clouds along with her and then moved back.

As I passed Midge's seat I saw that she was drawing on a big pad of paper. The open page was filled with sketches of dogs—big dogs, little dogs, smooth dogs, dogs with whiskers.

She glanced up at me. "All mine," she said. "I miss them so much. This is Chips. He's a boxer. This little guy is Willie. He's only got one eye but he doesn't miss a thing." Her voice was soft and full of longing.

"I don't know if I'll let myself get this far away from them ever again. Or from my husband," she added, giving me a grin.

Behind her, Geneva bobbed up and down in the back seat, mouthing "C'mon, c'mon" at me.

"You're a really good artist," I told Midge. "I'm going to be a writer. Maybe, when I publish my book, you could do the drawing for the cover."

"You're writing a dog book?"

"Uh-uh. A mystery," I told her. "But there may be dogs in it." I thought of the dogs that had jumped up at Stavros's bag. "I'm not exactly sure yet."

Midge nodded. "Let me know. I'm available."

I moved on back and slumped in the seat next to Geneva.

"So, what's this big idea you've got?" I asked her, trying not to sound miffed, which I have to admit I was. If the idea was good, I wanted to have been the one to think of it. In mystery stories there's a saying, "George must slay his own dragon," which actually means, the hero must do all the important stuff himself. And have the brilliant ideas himself. And solve the mystery. Still, I was a big enough person to at least listen. After all, till

I fired her, she was still my assistant.

"Well . . ." Geneva drew out the word. "Well, it's simple. You'll switch your bag with his."

I sighed. "Yeah? And how am I going to do that? You heard what he said on the raft?"

"What? What did he say?

"You didn't hear?"

She shook her head. "No. What was it?"

"He said, 'I will never let you go again.'" The words and the memory of the way he'd said them creeped me out all over again.

"How weird!" Geneva took off her cap and scratched her head. "Well, we're going to take it and he'll have to let it go. First, you will start carrying *your* bag everywhere. You'll put heavy stuff in it." She paused. "You did say his bag was heavy when you picked it up that time, in the bathroom?"

"Yep. And now I've seen into it. What's in there is definitely heavy."

Her mouth dropped open and that made me feel great.

"You've seen into it? Why didn't you tell me?"

"No time."

"And? And?" She pushed her face so close to mine I had to jerk my head back.

"It's something big and black and shiny." I paused. "And there's a string. I'll tell you this for sure. It isn't his puppy. And that string is not a leash."

"Why would he have a string?"

"It might be a fuse."

"Oh my gosh!" She was breathing through her nose, like a horse snorting. "A fuse? It's definitely a bomb, then. For inside the circle."

"Well, I don't know for sure. The big, black thing I saw didn't seem like—"

"Look, we've got to tell somebody! We can't wait any longer. This is too freaky—"

I interrupted. "First, let him read my letter. We'll see what he answers. You know, he might just say, 'I didn't mean to make a mystery of this. Here's my bag. Take a look inside.'" I sounded feeble, but I pushed on. "And I think we should examine Millie's picture before we do anything drastic. We'll see it tomorrow when we get to Yellowstone."

"We have no time to waste if we're acting alone," Geneva said. "We should tell your grandma. She's old. I bet she's wise."

"I don't want to worry her. And besides, she would be horrified that we're accusing him just because of the way he looks. She's *so* not into doing that."

"It's not only how he looks," Geneva said. "He has a bomb. He talks to his bag. How strange is that?"

I was getting irritated with her again. Miss Take-over, Run-the-show!

"We don't know for certain that it is a bomb," I said. "And I guess he can talk to his bag if he wants. It makes him a bit nutty, but nobody's going to arrest him for that. If you like, we could tell your dad," I added craftily.

Geneva gave me her murderous stare. "No way. I don't tell my dad anything, period. That way he would win."

"Win what?"

"Never mind," she said. "And I can't imagine telling Declan. He calls us 'kids.' Anyway, he'd never want to offend one of his customers. What would Star Tours say? Look at the way he gave in about Stavros's carry-on. On the raft."

"So it's up to us. I'll make the decisions," I told her. "George and his assistant will slay their own dragon."

She didn't look at me. She didn't seem to even hear me. "It's important then that we get the bag immediately," she said. "We could try to defuse the bomb ourselves. I bet *I* could. I programmed my mom's cell phone for her when nobody else could make it work. I'm pretty good with complicated stuff. So, after lunch, you fill your carry-on with heavy things, books, if you have any. Hey! There's a phone directory in my room, I can give you that."

"I probably have one," I said. "All this is fine. But how do we make the switcheroo?"

Geneva sat back with a satisfied smile. "You pack the bag. Bring it with you whatever we do this afternoon and I'll take care of the rest."

"How?"

"I know how. But I have a few details to work out. Like exactly when and where. That depends on him. I'll fill you in later."

Oh, brother, I thought. Did Sherlock Holmes ever have this kind of a problem with Watson?

CHAPTER

8

Before we left the bus that had brought us back to Jackson Lake Lodge, Declan came around to each of our seats.

I'd moved next to Grandma again, but Geneva had stayed in back.

"The schedule says you are at leisure this afternoon," Declan said. He had a clipboard and a pen. "But there are lots of things you can do here. I have a few suggestions, and I'm taking names. Or you may want to just hang out down by the lake, or up on the patio."

He glanced at his clipboard, which already had three short columns of names on it. "There's a boat ride on Jackson Lake. There's a nature walk, not difficult at all. And then there's an energetic hike, partway around the lake, that I'll be leading. This time of year we'll see lots of wildflowers."

"That last one sounds great," Grandma said.

"Good," Declan said. We watched him print "Mrs. Saunders" on his list.

While he was writing I squinted at the upside-down names in the three columns. I'm very good at upside-down reading, a trick I picked up from my best friend, Justin. It is a very useful skill when a teacher invites you to her desk to talk about your test paper or your homework that she has all marked up in front of her. It gives you breathing space to prepare your excuse.

Declan had been to Charles Stavros's seat before he came to ours. But I could upside-down see that Stavros's name wasn't on any of the lists. That meant he was hanging out at the lodge, which was dangerous.

"I think I'll just stay in the hotel," I told Grandma.

"Well . . ." Grandma sounded doubtful. "I don't

like you being here on your own, Kevin."

"Oh, Grandma," I protested. "There are tons of people. How could I be alone?"

Declan smiled. "Midge is staying. She wants to do some sketching, down by the lake. You could mention to her that Kevin's going to be around, too. He'll be fine."

"Okay, then." Grandma looked up at Declan. "What time?"

"Two-thirty. On the patio."

I turned to look at Geneva, who was still sitting alone in the back seat. She was twirling her rodeo cap on one finger, like a Frisbee.

"Excuse me," I said to Declan. "I'm just going to speak to Geneva."

I didn't appreciate at all the way he raised his eyebrows and gave me a sly little smile. What was he insinuating? He'd better not be insinuating what I thought he was insinuating.

I scowled at him as I pushed past.

"Geneva," I said, when I got to her seat, "Charles Stavros isn't going on any of the trips. We have to stay here, too."

Geneva looked up at me and beamed. "Perfect," she said.

"So?" I asked. "Are you going to fill me in on your plan?"

"Uh-uh."

"Have you ever heard of Mata Hari?" I asked.

"Uh-uh again."

"She was a spy and she was very mysterious. Everybody hated her. In the end she was executed. Do you think you're Mata Hari?"

"No, I'm Geneva," she said.

Before Grandma and I went to lunch I packed my red bag, as my assistant had suggested. But I was careful what I put in it. There were two phone directories in my room, both pretty skinny. I guess there aren't as many people living up here as there are in L.A. Fortunately there was also a spiral-bound book telling of all the things the Jackson Lake Lodge offered: the room service, the spa, and so on. I jammed it in, too.

As I weighed the bag in my hand I tried to remember the few seconds I'd held Stavros's. Was it just about the same weight? I considered, and then I put in the Greek dictionary. Grandma might ask me anyway if I'd brought it.

I knocked on her door, and the minute she opened it, she reminded me.

"The dictionary for Mr. Stavros? I can tell how anxious he is to read your note. He was so pleased that you would take the time, Kevin." She gave me one of her special loving smiles and I felt like a weasel.

I tapped my red bag. "It's in here," I said. "Geneva's staying, too. I brought books and stuff in here, in case we want to read." The phone books? I thought. Sorry, Grandma!

Unlike Declan, Grandma did not look even slightly insinuating when I spoke Geneva's name and said I would be spending time with her. Grandma wouldn't.

"Well, have fun," she said. "But check in with Midge now and then. I called her room and she's okay with looking out for you."

"Okay," I said.

We went down for lunch.

Buffo and Blessing invited us to sit with them at

their table. They were wearing baggy khaki shorts and identical long-sleeved blue T-shirts, and their bright red hair stuck up in the same kind of wet-looking spikes. Mousse, I thought. She moussed his and he moussed hers.

They were cheery and hungry. I couldn't believe how much they ate.

"Blessing is such a lovely name," Grandma said warmly.

"Isn't it?" Buffo reached over and pinched Blessing's cheek.

"My real name is Mary Jo," Blessing said. "But when Buffo and I met, he said I was such a blessing in his life that he changed my name, there and then."

"That is the nicest story," Grandma said.

"He's like that," Blessing said. "Romantic. He brings me flowers."

Buffo went on spreading butter on his roll but his face was a little pink. "Be quiet, woman," he said gruffly, but the smile he gave her wasn't gruff at all.

I took a nice crusty roll for myself. Who would have thought! Buffo the romantic!

I glanced up then and saw Millie and Beth coming

into the dining room. They stopped at our table.

"Hello," Millie said. She looked directly at me and rubbed her hands together the way you'd do to get them warm. "Tomorrow, Yellowstone," she said. "I can't wait!" She spoke with such significance that Grandma and Buffo and Blessing stopped eating to pay attention.

"Something special is happening at Yellowstone?" Blessing asked.

"Very special." Millie gave me another knowing look. She was talking about the picture, of course. What she didn't know—and what I wasn't about to tell her—was that Yellowstone was inside the Big C. The thought of that made my bite of roll snag in my throat, just about choking me.

"You don't like the Tetons, Millie?" Buffo asked.

"Oh, sure," Millie said. "But Yellowstone is going to be more exciting."

Maybe more exciting than she thought.

Beth sighed. "Come on, Mil. Let's get lunch."

"Look!" Millie whispered, half turning. Charles Stavros and his red bag were making their appearance.

"Just you wait, 'enry 'iggins, just you wait," Millie

sang in a sinister, whispery voice.

"Pardon?" Grandma asked, but Beth had a grip on Millie's elbow and was steering her away.

Stavros sat at a table across the room from us.

"Have you noticed how closely he sticks to that bag?" Blessing asked in a low voice. "I think it's filled with money, millions and millions of dollars. You don't think he's someone we need worry about, Mrs. Saunders?"

"I do not," Grandma said in a tone that closed the conversation.

The waiter brought us refills on coffee and iced tea and we talked for a while and then rose to leave. I edged the dictionary out of my bag.

"I think I'll just give him this now," I told Grandma.

"Good idea," she said. "I wonder what he's signed up for this afternoon?"

I shrugged my shoulders as if I didn't know.

Stavros thanked me for the dictionary. I thought he looked supiciously at my red bag, but that was probably my guilty imagination.

"I don't have any plans for this afternoon," he

said. "So I'll do my translation from this and get it back to you by dinnertime."

"Okay." I stood there looking at him. He had a kind of assurance about him, a confidence. As if he needed nobody but himself. Writers are observant about things like that.

Yikes! I was probably staring. I was about to turn away when he said, "Kevin?"

I stopped. Panic filled me. What?

"Thank you for taking the trouble to write to me. I'll write back to you, in Greek, if I can figure it out. We can keep this going!"

His smile flashed white under the mustache and the dark eyes smiled, too.

Oh my gosh! "Cool," I said.

Let me out of here!

Geneva and her dad were sitting in two of the chairs in the big lobby, facing the wall of glass. There was an empty chair between them. Through the windows I saw the dance of sun on the lake, the deep blues and greens of the Tetons behind. A drift of birds swerved against the sky, their wings changing from gray to silver as they turned.

"They're like leaves," I told Geneva. "You know, when you see the underside of a leaf it's a different—"

Geneva gave me a blank stare. "What are you talking about?"

"Nothing," I said.

She lifted her foot and touched my bag. "You're all set?"

"Yes," I said. "I don't know for what, but I'm set."

"He's still eating lunch." She twitched her head in the direction of the dining room. "The plan is this: He's not signed up for anything today. So we watch him. And wait for our chance."

"To switcheroo?"

"Yep. Want to sit? This is a good stakeout place."

I gave Geneva a glare. Now she was talking *my* kind of detective talk, but there wasn't much I could do about it. I'd take some of her dialogue out when I wrote my book.

As I sat down her dad smiled at me and said, "How's it going, young man?"

"Fine." I settled the red bag at my feet.

He nodded and went back to his book. It was still *The Boer War*. Well, it sure was a thick volume. I was glad he had it, since his daughter was being such a jerk to him.

Geneva and I watched the dining room door.

Stavros came out and walked toward the stairs.

We were behind him.

He stopped to buy a newspaper.

We pretended to look at magazines.

We peered around the corner as he went along the corridor and into his room.

We wedged ourselves behind a soft-drink machine till he came back out five minutes later and then we followed him back up the stairs and onto the patio. He was still carrying his bag and my dictionary.

All the outside patio chairs were filled. He walked along the flower-lined concrete path and then down the steps and across the grass to one of the wooden seats by the lake.

"Come on," Geneva ordered. So we sauntered down and sat on the thick trunk of a fallen tree, almost next to him. I was glad to set my red bag on the path at my feet. Those skinny phone books were getting heavier and heavier.

Stavros saw us and nodded.

I nodded back and Geneva gave a little wave.

Midge was a little farther away, on one of the benches, her unopened sketch pad on her lap. She was gazing up at the mountains.

A man and a little girl came strolling along the path. Geneva and I sat in silence. I guess we were waiting for them to pass.

Beside me I could feel Geneva throbbing like a drum.

"Are you ready to tell me what's up?" I asked. "It's so not cool to keep your"—I was going to say "boss," but at the last minute I changed the word—"partner uninformed."

"You don't need to be informed," Geneva said. "What *you* have to do is this. When he's occupied, and leaves that bag of his on the bench where it is now, you have to grab it fast and leave yours in its place."

"But how will he be occupied? Do you mean you're going to create a diversion?"

"You could say that." She gave a nervous titter.

I looked at Stavros, and—oh no!—he had taken out my note, unfolded it, and opened the dictionary.

I went clammy all over.

"He's going to read—," I began, but Geneva said urgently, "Be ready!"

After a few minutes, she got up and walked to the edge of the lake, almost into the water, where little ripples washed in and out, clear as iced tea. Now she strolled along till she was right in front of where Stavros was sitting.

He had his head bent over the dictionary and he paid no attention to Geneva. Not until she yelled, "Help! Help!"

I jumped up. She'd waded in, way beyond the lake's edge, and now she was floating facedown, as if she were drowning. Her Cody Rodeo Queen cap bobbed beside her. One arm windmilled skyward.

Midge leaped to her feet. Two women, farther along the path, screamed and began running in Geneva's direction.

But Stavros was closer.

He sprang up, sprinted toward her, reached down into the water, and grabbed her arm.

I could hear her saying, in a small, blubbery voice, "I'm all right. I just slipped. Sorry to freak you all out." She was dripping, her sweatshirt black with lake water, her jeans plastered against her legs. She wiped her wet face with her wet sleeve.

And there was Stavros's bag, unattended for the first time, sitting on the bench where he'd rushed off and left it.

Could I do this? Could I? I had to!

YES!

I picked up my bag, ran over, changed it for his, ran back, and set his on the path where mine had been. The diversion and the switcheroo!

We had it.

Mission accomplished.

CHAPTER

9

A small crowd had gathered around Geneva. I could hear her protesting again: "I just slipped. It's nothing. Thanks for helping me, Mr. Stavros. I was only up to my knees and I swear I thought I was drowning."

The bag! I had it and this was my chance. Everyone was watching Geneva and no one was watching me.

I had to look in it right now before Stavros discovered the trade.

I grabbed the end of the zipper and pulled. Nothing happened. It was stuck. I glanced frantically at the group surrounding Geneva, including Stavros.

Then Geneva's father came rushing down from the patio. "What happened?" he shouted. "Is Geneva all right?"

"I think so." I shooed him off toward her the way you'd shoo a pigeon in the park. Go, go, go, my thoughts urged.

I bent over the zipper. Maybe I could force it. I gave it a humongous tug but—oh no!—it wasn't stuck. There was a small combination lock fixed so the zipper wouldn't open. I hadn't seen it there before. Had he bought it back in Cody? Or brought it with him? He definitely had something to hide.

I gave the lakeside group another nervous glance.

Stavros was hurrying back to the bench where my bag was waiting for him. Mine, not his. He'd see there was no lock and he'd know right away that the bag wasn't his.

I sat, frozen.

Geneva waddled and dripped up onto the path. Her hair was smeared across her head like yellow seaweed. I saw that her father had draped his tweed jacket over her shoulders and he was carrying her rodeo cap. Her gaze was fixed on the bag beside me.

My brain swirled with indecision. What should I do?

Stavros had picked up my bag from his bench. He was checking it out.

I stood, clutching his against my chest, the way he always did.

Mr. Jenson had his arm draped around his daughter as they hurried toward the hotel. I heard him ask, "Sweetheart? Are you sure you're all right?"

"I'm okay." Geneva turned back to look at me. "Are you coming with us, Kev?"

Stavros was heading straight for me, *my* bag under his right arm, *my* dictionary in his left hand.

"I'm dead meat," I muttered, and Geneva said "Uh-oh" and began walking faster toward the lodge. "I'm really cold," she said, and her teeth chattered so loudly I could hear them. Fake, I thought. She just wants out of here. No way does she want to have to face him.

"You need a warm bath, honey lamb," Midge told

her. Then, to me: "You stay away from the lake till I get back, Kevin. Your grandma will have my hide."

"Okay." Stavros was almost upon me.

I couldn't just stand there waiting for the axe to fall. Action! Action! A hero is never passive. Not in mysteries, anyway.

"Kevin!" I'd never heard an angrier voice.

I took off, running like an antelope along the path that curved around the lake.

"Kevin!"

I held the bag tight against me. If there was a bomb in here, it wouldn't be too smart to jiggle it.

Running, running.

Two women stood aside to let me pass. One had a cane. "Sorry," I muttered as I just about tripped her.

"Really!" she said, superoffended.

Stavros's boots pounded on the path behind me.

"Hey! You've got my bag!" he yelled.

It was like he was saying, "Stop, thief!" My heart thumped with fear.

One of the women shouted, "Stop! You've got this man's bag!"

I pistoned on. My brain cells were pistoning, too, asking where I was running to. What good was this? I'd have to give up the bag. Action is excellent, but not if it's stupid.

In front of me four people walked, strung across the path. I'd have to power on through them.

"Excuse me," I bellowed. And then I saw they were the Texans.

They all turned.

"Whoa, cowboy! What's up?" one of them asked.

I stood still, panting. "It's okay," I gasped. "Just—"

And then he was beside me. Stavros's jeans clung to his legs. His boots were not shiny anymore.

"We had a bit of a mix-up with the carry-ons," he said pleasantly to the Texans. He handed me my dictionary and my bag.

I unglued his bag from my sweaty self and held it out to him. I couldn't think of another thing to do.

Mission abandoned.

"Did you go in the water, Mr. Stavros?" one of the Texan women asked, sounding incredulous.

Stavros smiled. "Only momentarily."

"Jim-dandy, then," another Texan said. I didn't

know his name. I didn't know any of their names. They strolled off and I stood staring down at my own carry-on as if I'd never seen it before.

"How did that mix-up happen?" I asked in the world's most dodo-brained voice.

Stavros didn't answer. Instead he pointed to a bench and sat down. When he nodded to the space next to him I sat, too.

"I think I know exactly how it happened," he said. For the first time I noticed that his eyebrows were almost as thick as his mustache. From underneath them his eyes watched me carefully.

He knew all right. He knew. This was so not good.

I was suddenly petrified. Here I was, sitting with a possible terrorist who knew I suspected him.

"I've read your note," he said.

My insides curled up small. Worse and more worse.

"I decided I would just answer you in English. No need to play the translating game." He stroked his bag with his bandaged hand and I saw that the bandage was still dry. He'd used the other hand to grab

Geneva. That was why he'd had to leave the bag behind. I was noticing these details but my mind was fussing about, not wanting to absorb what he'd said. He'd read the note. He was going to answer me.

I turned the dictionary round and round in my hands, examining it as if it were the most interesting thing I'd ever seen. A sideways glance told me that he was looking at a line of ducks dappling along the lake.

"You asked a question," he said at last. "And then I guess you decided not to wait for an answer. You needed to find out for yourself."

"I suppose." I took a quavery breath.

"Inside this bag," he said, "is something private and precious. It is not something I want to share." He faced me but I kept examining my dictionary, leafing through its tissue-paper pages, then partway opening and closing the zipper of my bag, which sat like an accusation between us.

"Don't you have some things that are private and precious to you, Kevin? Things you don't want to share?"

"Not really." An ant was chasing another ant across my knee and I moved my attention to them.

"The bottom line is," Charles Stavros said softly, "the bottom line is, it's none of your business what I've got in my bag."

"Okay." I dared to look up at him. "Of course, if you told me, I wouldn't tell anyone else." How nutty! Like if it was a bomb he was going to tell *me*.

He stood up. "I'm not about to tell you. Just don't try to steal my bag again."

I was insulted. "I wasn't stealing it."

"Just don't try it again."

And he was gone, holding the bag firmly against him, striding across the grass.

I felt as if I'd had a narrow escape. After all, he could have forced me up on a cliff and pushed me over. Just knowing I suspected him could have been enough to set him off. At the very least he might tell Grandma what I'd done. Terrorists are ruthless.

If he *was* a terrorist!

CHAPTER

10

The next morning, in the bus on the way to Yellowstone National Park, I told Geneva, "He seemed okay, close up and talking like that. He sounded cool. I'm beginning to wonder if we've made a mistake. If he isn't a terrorist at all."

"Are you kidding?" Geneva opened her navy blue eyes so wide, I was afraid they might pop out. "Give me a break! You're forgetting September eleventh. You're forgetting the way he looks. The way he guards whatever is in that bag with his life, almost."

"It's private and precious," I said. "That doesn't

sound like a bomb. And look, my paper scrap was still in his door this morning. He didn't go out all night. And we've watched his every move. Of course, we're not in Big C territory yet."

Geneva exhaled a long exhale. "I have a question for you. Why would anyone bring something super-private and precious on a bus tour? Wouldn't you keep it in a safe or somewhere? At home? And who *locks* a carry-on? I tell you, I don't trust him one bit. Remember, America trusted everyone, just about. Now we don't trust."

She was actually speaking so forcefully that little spatters of spit landed on my face. I wiped them away unobtrusively.

I could almost hear Grandma's voice. *She's right. We don't trust anymore, and that's the saddest thing of all.*

"You *want* him to be a terrorist, don't you," I said.

"I want to *catch* a terrorist," Geneva said. "So do you. If he is, and we uncover him, and stop him, we'll be heroes. Probably Oprah will want us on her show. Probably we'll get to go to the White House—and each get a medal."

I shrugged and stared out the bus window. Even a detective sometimes has to admit he's made a mistake. Maybe I had. Stavros had seemed so normal when I talked to him. So sane.

We were passing Jenny Lake, the sky and water the same color, the mountains shining behind it. Little boats rippled across it, leaving foaming wakes.

"It's like a picture postcard." Declan spoke through his minimike. "I never tire of looking at it." He told us about the famous geologic wonders we'd be seeing in the park. "Restless geology," he called it, because of the thundering waterfalls and the geysers and the bubbling mud pots.

I looked up the aisle at Charles Stavros's head and shoulders. He was looking out of his window, too. What was he thinking? That he should talk to Grandma about me? Or about his mission. If he for sure had one.

Behind him were Millie and her sister. "Not long now," she'd whispered to me as we boarded the bus. Would we recognize Charles Stavros in her picture of suspected terrorists? She was positive now. She'd thought about it, she told us. She'd brought the newspaper picture into focus in her mind and she was positive.

My grandma was sitting next to Midge. They liked each other, I could tell. They'd exchanged e-mail addresses for when they returned home.

Buffo and Blessing had been lying in the aisle, doing push-ups and leg lifts, bouncing up each time Declan drew our attention to something we were passing. Now they were back in their seats.

The Doves had their little gray heads together. They always seemed to have a lot to talk about, which was pretty amazing, considering how many years they'd spent together.

The Texans were laughing and calling out to each other—the Texans in their own space, as usual, taking no notice of the rest of us. They were playing some sort of word game. Sometimes one of them would shout, "Guilty! Guilty as sin!" or "Let that man go. He has a watertight alibi." I knew none of this had to do with Charles Stavros, but I began playing my own game. I closed my eyes and decided that whatever one of them called out next would be a sign as to whether Stavros was guilty or innocent.

"Hung jury!" one of the women announced.

Thanks a lot.

Geneva's father sat alone.

I finally decided to ask her. "How come you don't like him?" I said.

"Don't like who?"

"Your dad. He's always nice to you. He was really worried when he thought you were drowning in the lake."

Geneva made a face. "You're asking why I don't like him?"

I nodded.

"Well," she said. "If you must know, he and my mom are fighting over me like . . . like two wolves over a rabbit."

"What do you mean?"

"Oh, it's one of those miserable divorce things. They want to share me."

"Hard to believe," I said, and got one of her Geneva-cold stares.

"The judge says I'm old enough to decide. But when I said I didn't want to spend any time with my so-called father he ruled I had to go on this trip with him so we could get acquainted with each other. As if I want to."

"He seems like a nice guy—," I began.

"Like you would know," Geneva said. "He left my mom and me to go tend to all those, quote, distressed people in Africa. He didn't care at all about us. My mom asked him to come home but he said he'd made a commitment. He was needed. These were human beings. They had to have water if they were to grow their crops. He was bettering their lives. So arrogant!"

"Is that what your mom said? That he was arrogant?"

"That's what she said. And it's true."

I raised my eyebrows. "Well—"

"Now he wants to, quote, be a part of my life. The dam he helped build is supplying water to the towns and villages. There are other engineers there now. He wants me to spend Christmas vacation with him, and summer vacations, part of them, and some weekends."

"Well, he *is* your father. And how do you know he didn't care at all about you?"

"My mom told me."

I thought about that. "Does your mom like him?"

"No way." Geneva spoke quickly. "Not anymore. And now she has Eli and they . . ." She stopped.

"Maybe you and your mom could have gone to visit your dad," I suggested. "In Africa. Didn't he ever come home to visit you?"

"Sure. Big deal. Two weeks." She was staring out of the window, her shoulders hunched. "I never knew him, hardly."

"You could get to know him now . . . a bit. Maybe that's what the judge thought. You're being so not reasonable."

"Just quit it, okay? Mind your own business."

That was what Charles Stavros had told me. More or less.

Scotty had stopped the bus and we were disembarking to see the mud pots. We walked on a path between the gurgles and plops of the bubbling mud.

"Don't go near the edges," Declan warned. "We haven't lost a tour member yet."

"There's always the first time," Buffo cracked. He pretended to step into one of the small, steaming craters.

"This place stinks," Millie said. "If you ask me, it's like hell."

"The smell is sulfur in the form of hydrogen sulphate gas," Declan told us. "The temperature inside one is around one hundred eighty degrees Fahrenheit. The big one over there is called the Dragon's Throat. You can see why." Steam and stench hissed out like rotting beast-breath.

I walked behind Grandma. Not that I thought she'd fall in or anything. We kid around that she looks out for me and I look out for her.

I loved the mud pots. I'd never seen anything like them. But they were scary, too. Witches' cauldrons.

The high school kids had put on the play *Macbeth* last year. "When shall we three meet again? In thunder, lightning, or in rain?" the first witch had chanted. It wasn't hard to imagine the three witches stooped over these cauldrons in the dark of some wild night. "Fair is foul, and foul is fair." I shivered and stuffed my hands deep in my pockets. Too real!

"Do you think it looks like this on the moon?" Grandma asked, stopping for a second to stare across the bubbling landscape.

"Mars, more likely," Mr. Dove said from somewhere in front.

I kept my eyes on Stavros.

He walked along the circle of the path making no attempt to do anything sinister with the red bag that he held so securely. His private, precious bag.

I had this hollow feeling in my stomach as I looked at him. Maybe he wasn't a terrorist. I had wanted him to be, because of the way he looked and because of my book. But maybe, like Geneva had said, I wanted the glory. I should just wait till I saw Millie's pictures. And till I got a good look at that black, shiny thing and made sure it wasn't a bomb.

I should just wait. But more than anything, I hated waiting.

CHAPTER

11

We would be staying at the Old Faithful Inn in Yellowstone National Park for the next two days. You can't see the famous geyser from inside the inn. Declan told us that the architect who built it, way back when, planned it that way so that visitors would immediately see the geyser when they drove up the road to the front doors in their carriages. Of course, there isn't that much to see if it isn't shooting up its big column of water at just that time. But sit in your nice fancy carriage and wait a little while. Old Faithful "blows" every ninety minutes or so and it never fails. That's where it gets its name. There's a semi-nasty joke about laxatives and Old Faithful being "regular," but I won't put that in my book. There are tons of other geysers around in Yellowstone, but none is as big or as famous. Declan explained to us how it works. Water seeps down into porous rock, heats, and then rises back up as a geyser.

Declan told us the doors of the hotel were painted red, the color of welcome. "Mrs. Dove and I are going to paint ours red soon as we get home," Mr. Dove announced as the bus stopped to let us out.

"What a lovely idea." Mrs. Dove clapped her little hands. She is so all-time cute. Like Grandma.

We were in the lobby now, inside the inn, and it was all flagstones and wooden walls and wooden beams and wooden balconies held up by tree trunks as big around as telegraph poles. A monkey could go crazy in here.

"It's one of the biggest log buildings in the world," Declan said, so proudly you'd think he owned the place.

Millie had gone right to the front desk and was already deep in conversation with one of the clerks. I knew she was asking about the photograph from the paper that her friend was supposed to send her. The clerk left and came back with a big brown envelope. I edged closer.

"Miss Millie Yokomata?" he asked. "Yes. This came for you. By fax yesterday evening."

"Thanks a million." Millie beamed at him and sighed happily. When she turned I saw that she was wearing a sweatshirt with a dancing moose printed on the front. She looked like she might start dancing herself.

Geneva whispered to me, "She's got the photograph from the newspaper. I'm so stoked."

"Better not ask her about it now," I said. "She couldn't open the envelope down here, right in the lobby."

But of course she could. This was Millie.

She went across to one of the big wooden armchairs by the fireplace, ripped open the envelope, and bent her head over it. Her sister hovered next to her.

By now Declan had given us our keys.

"Millie?" he called, dangling a key with a tag on it above his head. "Beth?"

"I'll take it to them," I offered quickly. "They're reading a message that was left for them."

He tossed the key to me.

"I'll take it, too." Geneva hustled over beside me.

"Better not," I whispered. "Looks obvious. We don't want everybody crowding around."

She slitted her eyes. "Who made you the boss?" she asked. Her eyes didn't look a bit attractive, slitted like that.

"*I* made *myself* the boss. Relax." I stole a look at Charles Stavros. "Besides, we still have to watch him, just in case."

"So, do it yourself, boss," Geneva said coldly.

Declan was holding up a key. "Mr. Stavros? Two thirty-four."

Two, three, four. That would be easy to remember.

"I'll be up in a minute, Grandma," I said. "You go ahead." And I sauntered over to the big wooden armchair, now filled by both Millie and Beth, who were examining a sheet of photographs together. This could be it. The answer to who Charles Stavros was and what he was doing. No more wondering. No more guessing. I was tight with excitement. Or maybe dread.

From here I could see it. Eight little squares, each as big as half a graham cracker, marched across the paper.

The pictures were upside down to me. And although I have mastered the art of reading upside down, photographs are beyond my ability.

I moved behind their chair. The pictures weren't too clear, probably because they'd been copied from a newspaper clipping.

The men looked like they had been standing in a police lineup, straight out of a program on TV. The suspects behind the glass, the witness looking in, calling out, "Number three." And the police officer or the lawyer or someone asking, "Are you sure?"

Millie stabbed her finger at a picture of a man, only his head and shoulders showing. "Here he is! Look!" He had dark hair, a mustache, and a grim expression. To me he didn't look like Stavros at all.

"No," Beth whispered. "But *this* might be him." She pointed to the first guy in the lineup.

Millie shook her head. "Could be this one.

Imagine a mustache on him, and more hair." Her voice had gone flat. "Could be any of them."

"Could be none of them," I said. "Look at the names. There's not a Charles Stavros in the bunch."

"He might have changed it." Millie swung around to look at me.

"I don't think so," I said firmly, though I'd thought that very thought a few days ago. I'd been more suspicious a few days ago.

"I told you this was all rubbish." Beth tossed back her blacker-than-black hair and squeezed herself out of her tight spot beside Millie. Her little silver-ball earrings bounced and jiggled.

Millie glared. "One could still be him. The trouble is, they all look alike."

Beth sighed. "Oh, Millie. Just listen to yourself."

I was listening to her. It's a good thing my grandma wasn't. I'm not sure what she would have said to Millie, but it wouldn't have been pretty.

"What kind of a thing is that to say, Millie?" I asked. "He's not in the picture and that lets him out. Wherever you saw him before, it wasn't here."

"How would you like it if people said all

Japanese-American women look alike?" Beth asked. I was beginning to think of her as "Beth, the good sister."

Millie scowled. "Well, we don't. So they wouldn't."

I handed over their key.

Then I glanced up, and there he was. Stavros— looking at the fireplace and the humongous clock that hung over it, then turning to stare up at the beamed ceiling that stretched way over our heads.

"Quick!" Millie snatched the photo sheet from Beth, who'd been holding it, and stuffed it back in the envelope.

"Miss Yokomata and Miss Yokomata." Stavros nodded pleasantly at them and then at me. I noticed that the bandage on his hand wasn't so white anymore. Hadn't he said something about getting the hand rebandaged in Cody, which was our next stop? As always, he held the bag clasped against his chest. Now that I knew about the padlock, I saw its small, silvery gleam.

"Don't you get tired, carrying that bag around everywhere?" Millie asked brightly. "I ask only because our nephew, Billy, has to carry this colossal backpack with all his books in it every single day. Everywhere he goes in school, from class to class. They have no lockers, which I think is unconscionable."

I held my breath.

"I don't get tired," Stavros said.

"Maybe yours isn't as heavy," Millie said. "You want me to help you carry it?"

"Thanks," Stavros said. "I'm fine."

"Okay then." Millie sounded defeated.

Stavros laid his bandaged hand against one of the fireplace rocks.

"How is your hand, Mr. Stavros?" Beth, the good sister, asked.

"I think it's doing quite well, thanks," Stavros said.

"Not too painful?"

"Not anymore."

Stavros stepped back and looked all around. "Lodgepole pines," he said. "I'm glad the inn was spared in the big Yellowstone fire of 1988. This place would go up like a tinderbox. All this wood."

"Did you hear that?" Millie asked breathlessly as Stavros left us and headed for the stairs. "Maybe he's

131

an arsonist. An arsonist-terrorist. Oh wait, how about if he's going to blow up this inn? It's a . . . an American historical monument." She stopped. "No, I like the fire idea better."

"Like he's going to talk about a fire if he's an arsonist," I said.

Millie's face screwed up. "You know, I did see his picture. Somewhere. That's for sure. So what if it wasn't one of these? It was in the *Times*. I'm certain about that."

Beth groaned. "Sure. He's an arsonist. And he's been carrying matches and a can of gasoline with him from home. Get over yourself, Mil."

"I've got to go," I said quickly.

I wasn't sure what I felt as I went up the stairs to find my room. Millie had made me ashamed. No trust, Grandma had said. Man, was she ever right. But I had this other feeling. I was definitely disappointed. Let down. All the jazz had gone out of me. Without Charles Stavros to suspect, my mystery had fizzled. And without my mystery, well, it was still a nice trip but that extra interest was gone. Now I'd have to make up something for my novel. You just don't find mystery plots lying around; you have to think and plan and work them out. Joan Lowery Nixon probably didn't really know a girl like the one in *Shadowmaker*. Or one like Jenny in *Murdered, My Sweet*, which I'm reading now. I bet she made them up.

Buffo and Blessing were coming down the wooden staircase. They were in their shorts and running shoes and they had identical red sweatbands around their identical spiky red hair.

"Beautiful outside," Buffo boomed. "Can't waste time lollygagging around in a smashing place like this."

"Right," I said, and then I saw Charles Stavros standing at the top of the stairs, looking over the lodgepole railings, gazing down at the lobby below. He had set the red bag at his feet and was opening and closing his unbandaged hand, flexing his wrist.

He saw me and gave a half smile. "Miss Yokomata was right," he said. "As you know, my bag does get heavy after a while."

I took a deep breath. It was hard to decide if I was still suspicious of him or not.

But before I could gather my thoughts he lifted

the bag again, glanced at the number on his key tag, and said, "If I had two working hands, it would be easier. I could switch over, you know?"

I nodded.

"But never mind," he said, and now he spoke so softly I could hardly hear him. "Before long it will all be over."

Are you talking to me? Are you talking to me?

What would be over?

Inside me, things had started fizzing again. My ears tingled like crazy.

Now I knew for certain-sure that Stavros was up to *something*.

★ ★ ★

CHAPTER

12

★ ★ ★

B*efore long it will all be over.*

The words tumbled in my head as I went quickly past Grandma's room without even stopping, fumbled for my key, and unlocked my door.

I tossed my carry-on onto the bed. My mystery notebook was in my suitcase, which hadn't come up yet from the lobby.

I grabbed a sheet of Old Faithful Inn notepaper from the desk and printed those seven words in block letters. It's strange how writing things down makes them clearer. And truer. And scarier. What had Charles Stavros meant?

I stood staring at the paper and then, underneath his words, I wrote:

He might have meant our trip would soon be over. We just have Cody, the dude ranch, Mount Rushmore, and Rapid City, South Dakota. Those are the places left on our trip, the places inside the Big C. That might have been the only reason he circled them.

And that was the logical answer to the meaning of those words. But there could have been other meanings. I sucked on the pencil eraser (which is a very bad habit I have), then wrote:

Before long it will all be over.

Because???

a) The trip is almost over, or

b) He's going to give the bag to someone, or

c) He's going to leave the bag somewhere, or

d) He's going to stop carrying it around.

I tried to remember the tone of his voice as he spoke. Not angry. Not pleased. Almost tired, as if he'd come to the end of a long road.

My heartbeat was so loud I thought I could hear it.

My last possibility, the absolute worst one, was, *He's ready now to detonate the bomb.* But where? When?

I put my head down on the desk and took a shuddery breath.

The worst one, and one that was absolutely possible.

Once Dad had told me that people believe what they want to believe. I also knew that a person was innocent till proven guilty. I'd read that in mystery novels a gazillion times. But what if "Before long it will all be over" was as creepy as it sounded?

"I'm on a seesaw," I said out loud. "I just don't know. But I know I need to tell someone."

I took the sheet of paper and my key and went back along the corridor.

Passing Grandma's room I knocked on her door and said, "I'm going downstairs again. Back in a couple of minutes."

Her voice came faintly from inside. "I'm about to get in the shower. Tell the bellman if you see him to hurry with the luggage."

"Okay."

Declan always gave us his room number when we

arrived in a new hotel. "In case you want to complain about something," he would say, rolling his eyes.

I was glad now for the information.

Number 32.

I slowed and took deep, even breaths. If I tell him, I thought, it's not on me anymore. He can decide if Charles Stavros is a risk or not. It was kind of a relief. Mystery writers always have the hero/detective solve the case. But people could die if I didn't solve this one in time.

What if Declan wasn't in his room?

But when I knocked he came to the door right away. He was wearing sweatpants and a navy T-shirt and white socks. No hat. Slightly bald head. He didn't even look like Declan without his big cowboy hat and one of his flashy shirts, but he was. He didn't seem particularly happy to see me.

"What's up, young Kevin?" He held the door open only a bit, I guess hoping whatever was up he could fix with a word or two.

"May I come in?" I almost stuck my foot in his door. He'd better let me in, that was all.

"Sure, kiddo." He stepped back.

His room was small and not as nice as mine. Not that I'd seen mine for more than a couple of minutes. He waved me to the only chair and perched on the bed.

"So, what's the problem?"

I gulped. "It's Charles Stavros. I think he has something—something dangerous—in his Star Tours bag. You know the way he carries it all the time? And when we sort of asked him, it was Millie who actually sort of asked him, although I did before and . . ."

I stopped.

Declan was looking at me as if he thought I'd gone wacko.

I got up and thrust the paper at him. "I'm worried, because this is what he just said. And I don't know what it means."

He read the words. His feet in their socks wiggled like two squirmy white rats.

"And you think . . . ?" he said at last.

"Well, I don't know. I thought I ought to tell you."

Declan rose, gave me back the paper, stood looking down at me where I'd collapsed again into the chair, and said, "You can stop worrying, my friend. I know what he's got in the bag. I know why he carries it around. I know why it will all be over soon."

"You do?" I was astonished.

"I asked him, too. Remember when he insisted on taking the bag with him on the raft?"

I nodded.

"I asked him about it after the raft trip. And he told me. I didn't appreciate the way he ignored my order. He told me that in Salt Lake City he'd bought a very expensive gift for a friend in Cody. The friend's a doctor and he's going to change the bandage on Charles's hand. He says he bought a one-of-a-kind piece of Native American pottery. The gallery wrapped it pretty well but he doesn't have any kind of insurance on it in case it gets broken or stolen, and we don't, either." Declan spread his hands in a helpless gesture. "So he takes it with him—even on a raft."

"I'd think carrying it everywhere would be riskier," I said.

"He carries it very care-ful-ly." Declan drawled the words out like some kind of comedian.

"You know, I saw inside that bag," I told him. "It didn't look like Native American pottery to me. There was a black string thing."

"Could be the wrapping for the pottery piece has a string around it," Declan said. "And I'm not saying he hasn't got something else in there with it. He probably has."

"Something private and precious?" I asked.

"What?"

"Nothing. Have you noticed he keeps it locked?"

"I've noticed. That's his prerogative—that means his choice."

I thought it wiser not to say I knew what "prerogative" meant. "Can't you just ask him to open the bag for you? Tell him that you need to examine what's inside?"

"No way. I don't have the right to go looking in our guests' private luggage. How would you like it if I said, 'Kevin, open that bag of yours. I want to see what's inside.'"

I shrugged. "You can if you want."

"Your dirty laundry? No thanks." Declan grinned.

I stood up. "Well, I've told you."

"And you should have. That's what I'm here for." He put out his hand for me to shake, which I did, man to man.

He walked me to the door. "Have you seen Old Faithful yet?" he asked. "She's just about ready to blow. Check the notice in the lobby when you go through. They keep the times posted by the front desk."

I nodded.

Well, I'd told him and he'd given me an answer. But did I believe it?

CHAPTER

13

Grandma and I walked out to watch Old Faithful blow and it was something to see against the night sky. I wondered if a blue whale's spout went that high. We ooh'd and ah'd and cheered with everyone else.

"Way to go, Old Faithful!"

Charles Stavros watched, too, sitting alone on one of the benches, the red bag on his lap. Once I thought I saw his lips move and I imagined him saying to the bag, "I'm glad you could see this with me. Enjoy it, because now it's almost over."

My own imagination could make my skin crawl.

Dinner at the inn was great, but I had the most miserable, jumpy, nerve-racking night, checking on the paper scrap I'd wedged again in Charles Stavros's door. I was up so many times that at the end I think I was sleepwalking. No devoted assistant to help me.

"I'm on the other floor," Geneva had said. "I can't go walking around the corridors and up and down the stairs in the middle of the night." She'd given me that honest navy blue stare. "Sorry, Kev!"

Yeah, sure.

The next day we spent touring Yellowstone National Park. That is some big park! Declan says there are over 10,000 hot springs within its boundaries. We didn't see all of them, but we sure saw a lot. Two-thirds of the geysers in the world are located here. I have to say Declan keeps us well informed.

All the time I was admiring these natural wonders, I was keeping an eye out on Stavros, who seemed as innocent and interested as the rest of us. I tried hard to stay awake and not miss anything, but it's possible

I overlooked a couple of those hot springs.

We were back at the inn in time for dinner. I ate a lot because I wasn't going to get much sleep and I needed to keep up my strength. I'd tried cajoling Geneva again into helping me keep watch on Stavros, using the same paper-scrap-in-the-door trick, but I'd had no success.

"Thanks a whole lot," I'd told her. But sarcasm got me nowhere.

Three times that night I got out of bed and stumbled along the corridor to check that Stavros was still in his room. He was. The paper scrap was still in place, exactly where I'd put it.

It was maddening to think of him, the bad guy, in there sleeping peacefully all night long. Life is definitely not fair.

The morning of day seven, we were on our way to Cody. Historic Cody, Wyoming, founded by Buffalo Bill in 1896.

More of Declan's good information.

I sat with Grandma. I was dozing and pondering, pondering and dozing, and she was letting me.

My grandma knows when to talk and when a guy

needs quiet to think.

In front of me was Charles Stavros, his bag on his lap. Behind me were Geneva and her dad. Last night Grandma and I had sat with Midge at dinner, and that was part of my ponderings. Midge had been telling us about a dog she had in her kennels. A rottweiler.

"People are scared of rottweilers," she said. "No one has ever wanted to adopt Bogie and he's the sweetest dog you could ever imagine. And then we have another that *looks* like a rottweiler, but isn't. One glimpse of him and people shake their heads. Even looking like a rottweiler is bad news."

"That's the way it works," Grandma said. "Everybody judges."

Well, I was judging Charles Stavros and I couldn't seem to stop. Maybe what he had in that bag was totally innocent. But . . . I squirmed in my bus seat. He hadn't *shown* Declan anything, had he? Seeing is believing. And I was pretty sure what I'd seen hadn't been any Native American artifact wrapped up and tied with string.

We were driving down winding mountain roads.

"Western Wyoming," Declan said. "Home of oil wells and cowboys." And then he got excited. "Look! See the cowboys, driving their cattle . . . to the left of the bus. Port side, everyone."

Scotty slowed to an almost-stop and we crowded to port side to see. There they were, straight out of a movie. That could have been John Wayne, herding his cattle to market. No chuck wagon kicking up dirt behind them, though. Nobody shouting "Git along, little dogies!" At least, not that I could hear from inside the bus.

I love those old movies.

In the bus, still cameras clicked. Video cameras roamed.

"Kevin," Millie whispered, close to my ear, "want to see something strange? Or not so strange? Beth and I have been looking over the pictures we've taken so far on the trip. We got them developed in the photo shop at the inn. Check them out."

"Better sit down, Kevin," Declan called from the front as Scotty revved the motor again. I slid into one of the empty seats and began riffling through the photographs. In a nanosecond Geneva was beside me.

"What have you got?" she whispered.

It didn't take me long to discover what I'd got. Twenty-eight pictures. There were the Doves, sitting on a wall at Jackson Lake; the Texans, the four of them posing sidesaddle on a log as if it were a horse, waving their cowboy hats at the camera; Buffo and Blessing, striding out of Great Salt Lake, seaweed wrapped around them like banners; Grandma and Midge on a bench, gazing at Old Faithful, which looked like a plume of smoke in front of them; Geneva and me on the pier, waiting to go on the Snake River raft trip, Geneva's dad, reading on the porch of the Jackson Lake Lodge; Scotty and Declan, posed in front of the coach. There were lots of Millie and Beth, lots and lots of the scenery, and the bison and elk. The faraway bear. Some casual shots and . . . not a single looking-at-the-camera view of Charles Stavros. In the group getting out of the bus his head was lowered. On the raft trip his back was turned, even though I remembered Millie calling, "This way. Smile, everyone."

"You can't get a good look at Stavros in any of them," Geneva said.

I nodded. "He doesn't want to be recognized."

We stared at each other.

"Stay here a sec," I told her, and I took the pictures back to Millie.

"Interesting," I said. "But maybe he's just camera shy. I've started to wonder if he's like Midge's rottweiler."

"What?" Millie said.

I shrugged. "Just because Stavros looks dangerous and acts different doesn't—"

Millie gave me a hard look. "I know he's dangerous, Kevin. Viscerally, I know."

I went back to sit with Geneva.

"Viscerally, Millie knows." I yawned a gigantic yawn.

"What's she talking about?"

"Viscerally, in her gut, she knows Charles Stavros is a terrorist."

"We know, too," Geneva said.

"Well, I'm not certain anymore." I faced her astounded stare and before she could get sarcastic with me I told her about my visit to Declan's room last night, about how he'd explained away Stavros's coddling of the bag, etc., etc.

"That doesn't convince me," Geneva said at last. "And it shouldn't convince you, either."

"I was almost convinced," I said. "Except . . ." I paused. "Stavros said something to the bag. Or whatever's in the bag. He said, 'Before long it will all be over.' I heard him."

Geneva sucked in her breath. "Wow! That must mean he's going to do something now, fast, soon, today, tonight. So it can be over."

"My thinking exactly," I said.

I nibbled on my knuckles as we drove through the outskirts of Cody.

Now, fast, soon, today, tonight! I thought. Has to be, since we only have three days left, not counting the day we fly home.

"He's supposed to get his bandage changed here in Cody," Geneva reminded me. As if I needed reminding. "If this doctor is his friend, they may be in the plot together. What if he goes into the doctor's office or hospital or whatever and comes out without the bag? Huh? What about *that*?"

"The passing of the bomb," I said under my

breath, and I was in full suspicion mode again. "We have to keep following him. We can't let him out of our sight for one minute."

We high-fived each other. That girl's hand was bigger than mine!

Cody is a really neat town, half Old Western, half updated style. There are art galleries and world-famous museums and Buffalo Bill memorabilia every-where. And of course the rodeo, which we'd be going to tonight.

Our bus was taking us first to the Buffalo Bill Historical Center because just about everyone wanted to see it above anything. Everyone except Charles Stavros.

Geneva and I dawdled and heard him say, "I'll join the group later. I have to get my bandage changed."

"Okay. But we'll be leaving for the rodeo at seven-thirty," Declan said. "We'll have dinner first, then meet here in front of the hotel."

"I'll be on time," Stavros said.

"Declan? Geneva and I aren't too interested in the center," I told him, which was another big lie. I really wanted to see that museum. It had a bunch of stuff from the Pony Express, and all kinds of real saddles and guns and bronze action figures of cowboys and Indians. But this was a sacrifice I had to make. "Geneva and I just want to bounce around the town," I added.

That remark brought on one of Declan's not-too-well-hidden smirks. "Okay by me if it's okay with your folks," he said. "Just be careful where you bounce to!"

Grandma said it was all right by her, but was I sure I really wanted to miss the museum? "It's the best in the West," she said. "I thought you'd be interested, Kevin." She sounded a bit disappointed in me, but she didn't try to change my mind.

I guess Geneva's dad said okay, too.

We let Charles Stavros get ahead of us, then trailed along at a slow pace.

We saw him stop at a doorway, push open the door, and disappear inside.

"C'mon, quick!" Geneva urged.

The brass plate outside the door said DR. MICHAEL RAFFERTY, GENERAL MEDICINE.

"The doc doesn't sound like a Saudi Arabian or an

Iraqi," I muttered and I was thinking, wouldn't it have been great if it had said "Doc Holliday"—the old-time dentist who was in so many shoot-'em-up Westerns? And what if we'd been standing here and the James brothers had ridden up and . . . ? But this wasn't then. And practically speaking, this could be worse.

"We can stand in this doorway and wait," I said. "They won't see us, since it's set back. But we can peer out and see them if we're careful."

"Okay." Geneva was enthusiastic and excited. "I think we're going to find out something, Kev," she whispered. "I have this feeling."

I had it, too.

But the longer we waited, the more Geneva's enthusiasm wore off.

"What's keeping him?" she muttered. "He just has to get a bandage changed."

"Maybe he's visiting," I suggested. "Isn't the doc supposed to be his friend?" And I thought, Maybe they're conspiring, talking terrorist talk, planning exactly where inside the circle to set the bomb. I was suddenly cold, though our little doorway, next to the doctor's, was fully in the sun. Of course, Stavros could be innocent. Declan thought so. He was having his bandage changed and gabbing with an old friend, that was all. I hated this "he is, he isn't." It was wearing me down. That and lack of sleep.

We waited and waited.

"I'm sick of this," Geneva whined. "We're missing the rest of the town. And we're not having fun."

"Detectives aren't supposed to have fun," I said. "This is a stakeout. This is our job. And it's a patriotic job, too. Think about being on the Oprah show."

Just then the doctor's door opened and Charles Stavros came out of the office. There was a man with him, bald on top but with a skimpy little ponytail. He was wearing a white coat. This I saw in one quick, secretive peek before I drew back out of sight, like a turtle into its shell.

Dr. Michael Rafferty, I thought. And his friend, Mr. Charles Stavros.

They were talking and it seemed like the middle of a conversation. I gripped Geneva's arm and strained to hear.

"You won't be able to get close," the doctor said.

"There's too much security."

"I'll get close enough. I've come all this way to do it and nothing's going to stop me now."

"Oh my gosh!" Geneva breathed.

I squeezed her arm. "Shh."

She was doing that snorting thing again, like she had a marble up her nose. I wanted to put my hand over her nose and mouth in case they'd hear her.

But they were talking again.

"At least be careful."

"I will."

I risked another peek.

They were shaking hands. "Well, thanks again for the vase. Good luck, Charlie."

I pulled back.

Geneva and I stared at each other. Her face was all shiny with sweat.

I heard the door close and Stavros's footsteps going away from us along the sidewalk.

We waited for about thirty seconds, then came out of our hiding place.

"I can't believe it," Geneva muttered. "This is *so* not believable!"

"I know."

Stavros walked purposefully along past the shops, and a thought I'd had before popped into my head: a man with a mission. I took a deep breath and tried to think.

He was still carrying the red bag. Was it a little less bulky? It should be if he'd given his friend the vase. But I was sure the main thing, the dangerous thing, was still in there. His bandage was smaller, fresh and dazzlingly white in the warm Cody sun.

"He's not going back to the hotel. Or to the museum," Geneva whispered. "He's headed for somewhere else. Kevin, I don't know if we can do this. This is . . . this is . . ."

"We can. We're onto him. There's no turning back."

Stavros was walking quickly now, slowing as he passed each store window or open door, checking inside. I deduced he was looking for a special place but he didn't know exactly where it was. Maybe Dr. Rafferty had given him some directions that weren't too precise.

He stopped suddenly, stood for a moment, and then went inside a store. I looked up at the sign over the door: CODY HARDWARE. ALL YOU NEED FOR RANCH OR FARM.

We sidled in.

The owner wasn't kidding. There was everything here you could possibly need, winter or summer, for a farm or a ranch. There were small tractors with the name John Deere emblazoned on their sides; there were snowmobiles. There were garbage cans and feeding troughs and bins that held flower bulbs or assorted nails and screws. Something for everyone.

Stavros was at the far end of the store.

Geneva and I hid behind a large barrel filled with pickles that smelled strongly of vinegar. Do people really buy pickles from a barrel anymore? And in a hardware store? I guess they do in Cody.

Stavros paced along one of the aisles, and as we watched he picked up something I couldn't see and carried it to the counter.

Geneva whispered, "What is it? What did he buy?"

My throat was so tight I could hardly answer. I

wanted to cough, just a little cough. But I didn't dare. What if Stavros looked over and saw us?

"It's a shovel," I said when my voice came back. "He's buying a shovel. And a flashlight."

CHAPTER

14

Geneva and I crouched behind the pickle barrel. She'd grabbed my wrist and dug her nails in. I pried her fingers off my wrist.

As the salesman wrapped the shovel in heavy brown paper, he and Stavros were having a conversation that seemed to be interesting and friendly. The shovel had one of those short folding handles, and it folded up to be not much longer than a baseball bat. Stavros set the red bag on the counter, moved his fingertips over the padlock, unzipped the top of the bag, and slipped the flashlight in. I saw him carefully relock the bag.

"Let's go," I whispered to Geneva.

We hurried out of the store and along the sidewalk. No need to keep watch on him right now. We'd seen all we needed to see. I had no doubts anymore. But I was pretty sure whatever he was planning wasn't going to take place on the streets of Cody. Not in daylight. Not with that shovel and flashlight.

Geneva and I talked so fast, our sentences crossed each other in midair, so mixed up I could hardly tell who was saying what.

"He's going to bury something."

"Or dig something up."

"You don't bury a bomb."

"Some bombs you do. There are bomb-sniffing dogs that can find them."

"Oh, man, I wish we had one of those right now!"

We kept tripping over our own feet as we looked back to see where Stavros was.

"He's coming. But he's a half block away," Geneva said.

"I know that. I can see, too, you know."

"Why didn't he bring the shovel and flashlight with him from home?"

"He couldn't. Security would have been on him. You can't board a plane with stuff like that."

"Because of terrorists." Geneva shivered, and I shivered with her.

"He said it was almost over. He's going to do it. He's come all this way from New York." I decided that every word Charles Stavros had ever spoken was engraved in my brain. "And Geneva," I said, "you absolutely have to help me watch him in the hotel. We have only three nights. No making excuses and bugging out. We're in the circle, the Big C. We have to be able to see his door every single minute."

"And if he comes out, and he's carrying the bag and the shovel and the flashlight? What do we do?" Geneva bit her lip and pulled her shoulders up against her ears. "Oh, man! If that happens, I hope you're on watch and not me. How do we stop him?"

"I'm thinking," I said. "Your dad has a cell phone, right? Do you know the number?"

"What do you think? Like I call him all the time?"

"But you could get the number. And I could

borrow Grandma's cell. She's let me before. Then we'd have a link. If things got really hairy, you could call your dad and—"

Geneva rolled her eyes. "Can't we link with somebody else?

"Who? The Doves? Midge? Millie?"

"Buffo," Geneva said. "He'd be great!"

"He and Blessing don't have a cell. Remember they were waiting to use the phone in the hotel? Anyway, your dad would be just as good as Buffo. Better. He loves you. If he thought you were in trouble, he'd—"

"Oh, sure. He loves me."

I didn't answer that. "Just get the number, okay?"

We were both quiet. Then Geneva said, "What if he decides not to go to the rodeo? Will that mean we can't go? I want to. I *really* want to"

"Me, too."

"But I've even got my rodeo cap."

We could see our bus waiting in front of the hotel, Scotty standing by the open door, and I didn't mean to quicken my steps and I don't think Geneva meant to, either, but suddenly we were walking so fast we were almost running. The bus and Scotty seemed so safe.

"Hi," Scotty said as we came closer. "Interesting town, Cody."

"Really," I said, and realized I'd hardly seen it. Only the inside of Cody Hardware. Maybe I'd never be in Cody again in my whole life. And I'd missed it. I'd missed the museum and all that cool stuff. But how important was that compared to saving whatever or whomever Stavros was after?

"Hop in," Scotty said. "I'm going to drive to the museum and pick up the others. Or you can wait here and get yourselves a soft drink in the hotel coffee shop. I'll be back in about twenty minutes."

I glanced over my shoulder. Stavros was only a few steps away, and I decided quickly. "We'll go on the bus with you." Geneva and I flopped into different seats.

"Here comes Mr. Stavros," Scotty said. "We'll hang on a minute and see what he wants to do."

Charles Stavros waved and climbed up the bus steps.

"We're just going up to the historical center, if

you want to come." Scotty looked at the long package Stavros was carrying. "Shopping, I see, Mr. Stavros. Shall I put that up in the rack for you?"

"Well . . ." Stavros hesitated. "Okay. I guess that will be all right."

He handed over the package but kept the red bag. "You skipped the center?" he asked Geneva and me.

"Yeah." My voice snagged in my throat.

"Too bad," he said pleasantly. "I hear it's a good one. Well, I missed out on it, too." He held up his bandaged hand. "But I did get this taken care of."

"That and more," Geneva whispered to me.

How could he be so calm, I wondered, planning what he was planning? He'd be a good villain in my book, in *any* book, no question. Two dimensional. Maybe even three.

Our coach lumbered up the street, made the loop in front of the historical center, and gathered our group back aboard. They lugged all shapes and sizes of gift bags.

"That visit was worth the whole trip," Mr. Dove announced. He carried a square, flat package. "Indian painting," he said. "Very powerful."

"Their gift shop was great," Midge told us. "I wanted to take something home for my dogs, but there are so many of them. So I bought this for my husband instead." It was one of those viewers that show places of interest. "Since he couldn't come," she added.

Geneva's dad walked down the aisle and handed her a small velvet bag. "I hope you like this," he said hesitantly.

She pulled open the drawstring top and trailed out a silver chain with a butterfly pendant of blue stones. The stones were all different shades of blues, some almost as dark as her eyes, some a pale blue-green.

Grandma saw it as she was getting into her seat. "Oh!" She put her hand to her throat. "That is absolutely beautiful, Geneva. All turquoise and so intricately set."

Geneva was very still, dangling the chain between her fingers.

"I know it's not your birthstone, Geneva," her dad said softly. "You are December nineteenth."

"Right," Geneva said. "But I love this. It's beautiful."

"And I know how you love butterflies," he said. "Do you remember when I took you to the Monarch Festival when you were, oh, maybe four? All those black-and-orange butterflies hanging from the trees and then soaring up, like a bright cloud?"

Geneva nodded again. She touched the pendant. "I didn't think you'd . . . remember the day with the monarchs."

I could tell she was almost crying.

Her dad touched her cheek. "Turn around and let me put this on."

She turned awkwardly in her seat. I watched him fasten the necklace in back and then, secretly, smooth the yellow tufts of her hair.

"Thank you," Geneva said.

I'm not a very mushy person, but I guess I am sort of a writer so I have feelings and intuitions. Right then I felt that Geneva was thanking him for the butterfly, but even more for remembering.

She suddenly got out of her seat, moved past me and past her dad, and sat in a seat by herself. I wanted to talk to her more about Charles Stavros and our plans for tonight, but this didn't seem to be the right time.

I moved in next to Grandma.

"Wouldn't it be fine if this trip brought the two of them together?" she whispered.

"Totally," I answered. I stared out of the bus window, past Grandma's head. Across from us Charles Stavros sat, detached as ever, the red bag close beside him, the red bag with the big flashlight and whatever else was in it. And, in the rack above his head, the shovel.

We were on our way now to dinner and to our hotel, which was outside the town.

"Don't worry. We're coming back in for the rodeo," Declan said. "First a real, honest-to-goodness cowpoke dinner, beans and ribs and fried chicken and biscuits. Three kinds of pie!"

There were whistles from the Texans, and Buffo said, "Shucks. Blessing and I can eat three pies all by ourselves."

"Anybody not want to go to the rodeo after dinner?"

I held my breath. Declan went around us inquiring.

Only one person was staying away. That one person was Midge.

"I don't think I could stomach it," she said. "I know those riders aren't supposed to hurt the horses and bulls they ride, but I have my doubts. How do you make a horse buck and toss like that if he isn't in pain? I've heard they put spikes under the saddles."

"Oh, dear." Grandma's face crumpled. "They wouldn't, surely?"

"The Cody rodeo's been going for more than fifty years," Declan said. "And I've never heard of any complaints from animal activists. Or the ASPCA." He sounded personally offended.

"Well, I might just be the first," Midge said. "The rest of you, enjoy."

It might not be so easy to enjoy after what she'd said, but I still wanted to see it.

I watched carefully to be certain Stavros was going. He was.

Geneva sat alone. I turned twice, and each time I saw that she was leaning forward in her seat, touching the turquoise butterfly that swung on its chain around her neck. I wondered what she was thinking. I hoped she'd still be able to concentrate on Stavros, too, because whatever he planned on doing was going to happen very, very soon. Time was running out. And what was *our* plan?

Dinner was great. There was everything Declan had told us about and more. Buffalo stew, gravy thick as pudding, steaming homemade biscuits. We were overstuffed as we groaned our way back to the bus, heading for the hotel, which was actually a fancy dude ranch: the Lazy Y.

Log cabins were scattered across the grassy grounds. Grandma and I and Midge and Stavros were in one of the smaller ones that Declan said had been part of the original house. The Doves, Geneva and her dad, and Buffo and Blessing were in another, and the Texans and Millie and Beth in the third.

Horses grazed peacefully in a meadow yellow with buttercups. There was a stream, and a pond, and tennis courts and an orchard. I think the trees were apple trees.

We had hardly any chance to look around. Declan had said we'd have time to enjoy it in the morning.

"Want to play tennis tomorrow?" Geneva asked.

"If we have nothing else to do," I said meaningfully.

The bedrooms were upstairs. Mine had a feather bed with a comforter on top, white and fluffy as a marshmallow. It looked so tempting. What were my chances of sleeping in it all night long? Not good. I wanted to crawl in it right then.

"Wake up!" I said out loud. "You can sleep when you get home."

I staggered into the little old-fashioned bathroom and washed my hands and face, rubbing my wet hands over my hair and into my scalp, massaging. "Vigilance!" I said. It was an excellent word that I remembered from a mystery novel. I said it again. "Vigilance!"

The mirror was old and blotchy, as if the surface was off here and there. In it I looked superstrange. Were my eyes really that sunken in? I propped my eyelids open with my wet fingers. Zombie eyes. I wondered who had lived in this house, and washed in this washbasin, and looked in this mirror. I was just beginning to freak myself out even more than I was already freaked when I heard the coach motor below. Rodeo time. I pushed aside the frilly curtains and peered out the window. I saw Millie slouching out from her cabin, smoking a cigarette. She took a last drag, then tossed the glowing butt into the bushes.

Charles Stavros came from nowhere. He was ready for the rodeo in his windbreaker and scarf. The red bag was clutched against his chest and he was carrying the pillow from his bed. Declan had told us we should take our pillows because the rodeo seats were so hard. Stavros was moving fast. I saw him shout something to Millie, something that I couldn't hear, but it wasn't hard to see he was ready to explode with anger. He pushed aside the bushes and stomped on the ground, all the time speaking over his shoulder to Millie, his face grim. When he came out of the bushes he was holding the squashed butt of her cigarette.

I eased the window open just a bit.

Now I could hear some of his furious words. "Crazy . . . Fire . . . Don't you know . . . ?"

Millie glared up at him, her hands on her hips. "Why don't you mind your own business?" Her voice was shrill, shaking with anger.

"It is my business. If you burn this place down . . ." He lifted her hand, jammed the flattened butt into it, then pushed past her onto the bus.

Quietly I eased my window closed and sank into the edge of my fluffy bed, wide, wide awake.

Stavros had been angry. More than angry. Furious. But there was something else. He'd been afraid. Afraid above normal. Afraid of fire.

What did that mean?

"Bring your warmest duds," Declan had drawled.

We were warmly dressed; we had our pillows and blankets. Prepared all the way.

I sat with Grandma, since Midge hadn't come. "I'm not sure about this anymore," Grandma said. "When I went with your grandpa, I thought the horses weren't being hurt."

"It's okay," I told her. "Remember what Declan said? This rodeo has been going on for a gazillion years. If it was really cruel, it would have been stopped long ago."

We walked from the bus, past the horses—the broncos—milling around in their pens waiting for the show. Past the humongous bulls, humpbacked, steamy-eyed, standing motionless as if ready to charge.

"You think they're going to ride those?" Grandma asked, and one of the Texans said, "They surely are, ma'am. And it will be something to see."

The air was rich with the smell of manure. I breathed it in. This was fresh, much nicer than the stale stuff we spread on our grass and flower beds at home.

Charles Stavros, complete with red bag, white bandage, and white pillow under his arm, walked in front of us. The shovel was still in the bus, in the rack where Scotty had put it. Why hadn't he left it at the hotel? I was getting creeped out again. Was he going to use it tonight, sometime, somewhere after the rodeo? I'd heard him ask Scotty twice if the coach would definitely be locked while we were watching the show and if Scotty would always be with it. Mr. Dove had been anxious, too, about his painting, which he wanted to leave in the bus till the end of the tour. That made sense. He didn't want to lug his painting in and out of the different hotels. But a shovel? Maybe it was like the bag: Stavros wanted it with him at all times in case an opportunity arose. Or until *the* opportunity arose. This thought put me on edge even more.

Scotty had assured Stavros and Mr. Dove and everybody else that their belongings would be safe. If Stavros didn't take that shovel out of the bus when we got back to the dude ranch, I'd feel a whole lot better. And safer. Maybe I'd even sleep. Let him leave it locked up so he couldn't get at it.

Stavros sat two rows in front of Grandma and me.

Geneva and her dad were right behind us on those hard bleacher seats. She was wearing her rodeo cap and her butterfly necklace. I heard her father ask her if she was warm enough and heard her answer, "Yes, thank you," in a voice that was nice and friendly for once.

Okay, I thought. Things seemed to be on the way to being possible for them.

I looked for Millie. She and Beth sat way at the other end of the row of seats in front of us. Once they got up and squeezed along the row in back of Stavros. Millie was smoking, and as she passed him she leaned forward, till her face was almost up against his, and blew a cloud of cigarette smoke in a blue haze around his head.

"So sorry," she piped sweetly, and then she turned all the way around and winked at me.

I didn't wink back. What a jerk she was!

The stands were crowded and there was so much excitement in the air you got excited yourself, just being a part of it. I'd never seen this many cowboys in one place, cowgirls, too, all dressed up to watch the rodeo in their fringed jackets and boots and spurs. I'd never seen so many junior cowboys, either, miniature versions of their dads and moms. Old country-style music blasted from loudspeakers. High above us the Wyoming night sparkled with stars that I could see even past the floodlights. Below us I could see the pens that each held a single fiery-looking, steam-breathing, gigantic bull. The chosen ones. Sometimes one threw itself at the rails of its wooden corral or stood up like some enormous wild beast, hooves thundering on the wood. Oh, man. What if one of them escaped?

Grandma said, "This is all so interesting," in the weakest voice imaginable.

And then a loud "HOWDY, FOLKS" came through the loudspeakers. "Welcome to Cody Night Rodeo, where the best compete with the best."

We'd started.

Stavros was looking intently down at the arena or ring or whatever. I promised myself that however exciting the show was, I wouldn't let him out of my sight or out of my mind.

It wasn't easy to keep remembering him. There was so much going on. There were cowgirls barrel racing, bent over their saddles, the flying hooves of the horses kicking up streams of dirt.

"Give a big hand now to Miss Annie Oakley," the announcer boomed. "I kid you not, folks, that's her name."

There was steer wrestling and team roping,

bareback riders and saddle bronc riders. There were clowns and calf wrestling. Each time one of the small calves thudded to the ground, bawling and screaming, Grandma would squeeze my hand and close her eyes.

I'd close mine, too.

"Do you want to go back and sit in the bus?" I asked her. "I'll go with you. Scotty will let us on."

But she shook her head and said faintly, "I keep reminding myself of what you said. If this was really cruel, it would have been stopped a long time ago."

"Right," I said, and squeezed her arm.

The horses came one by one out of the chute, which was a passageway from the holding pen, the rider already on, clinging with knees and feet, an arm waving for balance.

"Big show-off," Buffo hollered.

The horse would begin bucking and leaping, its only aim in life to get that rider off its back. Were they trained to do that? Or was there really something sharp under those saddles? I didn't know. But no rider lasted long. A few seconds and he'd be thrown, the horse tossing its head in triumph or relief.

When they brought out the first bull and its rider there were gasps of fear from the audience, even though probably most of them had seen this before. We hadn't. The bulls were massive, dangerous now as uncaged bears, shrugging the riders off, looking as if they'd pick them up on their long sharp horns. But the clowns with their red scarves tempted them away, the men and bulls racing together across the dirt, the second clown coming in to rescue the first, the stands erupting in applause.

Behind me, Geneva punched on my shoulders. "This is so great," she screamed in my ear. "I want to do this when I'm older."

"I just bet you could," I said.

Charles Stavros never left the stands. He never left my sideways vision.

Not even when we walked back to the bus, everyone chattering and prattling about what we'd seen.

Lugging our blankets and pillows we climbed aboard. I checked. The shovel was still in the rack.

Geneva and I sat together. She leaned toward me

and said, "213-555-3257," and I didn't need to ask what she meant.

I wrote her dad's cell number in my mystery notebook.

That was as ready as we could be for whatever might happen.

That night, when I figured everyone was asleep, I went down to the parlor of the cabin and lay on the hard settle, the marshmallow comforter over me and under me, Grandma's cell tight in my hand, 213-555-3257 transferred from my book into my brain. I'd brought my pillow but not my blankey square, because the comfort of it might drift me into sleep and that could be fatal.

There was a piano in one corner. Before we turned in, our group had joined in a singalong, led by the Texans. Stavros had mumbled the words to go with the tunes. I was interested that he knew them. They were all traditional American songs—like "She'll Be Coming Round the Mountain" and "Camptown Races." He didn't sing much, but he knew the words, all right. Sometimes he'd say a word or two off-key. The room was still warm and smoky from the fire we'd had while we were singing. High up, the ceiling beams were blackened from old heat; around the stove, the floor was pitted and scarred.

Light from an outdoor lamp on a tall pole shone through the window.

In front of me were the stairs that led to the bedrooms. I'd pulled a piece of black thread from the sewing kit in my room and tied it banister to banister across the bottom of the stairs. It was invisible but it would break if anyone crossed it. I hoped no innocent person would come down and trip. This thread trick had been in *One Thief at a Time*. The detective had put powder on the thread and the next day he'd seen a white line on the sweater of the man he'd suspected all along. But I only had one suspect, so I passed on the powder. And besides, either Geneva or I would be on watch. The thread was only a precaution so we'd know if—awful thought—we'd missed him. After tonight we'd have only two nights left.

I eyed the big metal poker that leaned against the

bench by the stove and fantasized about Stavros creeping down the stairs like a panther, me racing at him, brandishing the weapon, shouting, "It's over! We've got you!" When I imagined him he was slinking along in his socks, the red bag cradled against him, his flashlight in his hand, the shovel ready, and I'd rush at him out of nowhere and . . . But he didn't have the shovel. It was in the bus. And he must need it for whatever he was planning, because he'd bought it.

My alarm clock was under the comforter; it was set for 2:30, when Geneva was supposed to come and relieve me. She'd argued for 3:30 but I'd held firm.

I was swaying into sleep and I must have dozed because Geneva wakened me by poking me with an unfriendly finger.

"Oh, this is great!" she said, grumpy as could be. "He could have bombed us all and you would have slept through it."

I untangled myself from the comforter. "Give me a break. I was wide awake."

She plonked down beside me. "I'm sick of this. I was having a dream and I was in a circus and I was bareback riding on a pony—"

"Yeah, yeah, yeah." I yawned. "Be out of here by five. Ranchers rise early, and you don't want to be caught."

"All I can say is, he'd better be going to blow something up after all of this," she said.

I scowled. "Oh brother. You're something else!"

I have to say, Geneva didn't look too great. I almost wished the outside light wasn't so bright. Of course, it was 2:30 in the morning and she probably wasn't really with it yet. She was wrapped in a patchwork quilt. Her feet stuck out, red and cold, underneath. Her toes were really knobby and gross and her hair was like a dandelion with half the petals missing. I saw a glint of silver round her neck. The butterfly necklace.

"I'm off to bed," I said. "Be sure to stay on your guard."

"Hey, Kevin. Don't go yet. Let's talk for a while."

"That would be so not smart—"

"Please!"

She curled herself up on the settle, those totally gross feet tucked out of sight.

"Okay. Just for a minute," I said. "I'm supersleepy." Which wasn't exactly true. Since she'd poked me with that jabbing finger I was wide awake. I cocooned myself in the marshmallow comforter beside her.

"Suppose, just suppose, he doesn't have a bomb in that bag?" she asked, staring at me. Her eyes were that depthless dark, dark blue.

"Are you kidding? What else could he have? It's a bomb, all right." I couldn't believe she was saying this now.

"But he did say it was something precious and private. That's what confuses me. Would you call a bomb precious and private?"

"No. But I'm not a terrorist and he is."

We sat in silence. I wondered if the cows we'd seen in the pastures outside were asleep in their cozy barn. The horses. The chickens.

"Do *you* have something private and precious?" Geneva asked.

"Naw," I said, lying.

"I bet you do. I bet everybody does. I do. And if you tell me, I'll tell you."

I considered, semi-intrigued. "You first, then."

"No, you. I had the idea. I get dibs."

"It definitely has to be you first," I said, telling myself that I'd pull out if hers was something stupid. She'd probably think mine was stupid anyway.

"Okay, then. But you'd better not weasel out." She bent her head.

"So, what is this private, precious thing?"

"These." She lifted her cupped hands and in them I saw something shining and silvery.

"What are they?"

"My contact lenses. They're what make my eyes so pretty. I never tell anyone because my eyes are the only pretty things about me." She looked straight at me and I couldn't believe it. The dark blue color had disappeared and I was looking into a pair of pale, washed-out, ordinary, anybody eyes.

"Oh my gosh!" I said, remembering how many people had complimented her, even Grandma.

"I'm really ugly," she said.

I sat up straight. "No, you're not. Except for your feet. I bet some guys would even think you're okay-looking." I struggled to find something else good to say. "You've got great hair. It's like . . . like a rock star's."

"Really?"

"Yeah. I mean it."

She bent forward and I guessed she was putting her contacts back in. "Okay," she said. When she straightened, her eyes were dark and beautiful and mysterious again. "Your turn."

"I was thinking maybe you don't want to know what—"

"I do. And you promised."

"Okay." I pulled the marshmallow comforter up around my face as much as I could without actually burrowing into it. My voice was muffled.

"I have a blankey square."

"A what?"

I let the words come in a rush so maybe she wouldn't hear them right. "It's a corner of the baby blanket that I used to have, and I take it with me places where I have to sleep, and I put it on my pillow and I know it's seriously stupid and babyish and nobody knows except my mom and maybe my dad and . . ." I finished, "And now you."

I could feel her considering. "That's not so bad. I definitely expected worse. But I can see why it's private. Your friends would for sure think you were a bozo."

"Thanks," I said.

"Well, I don't think that. When my dad was away, I sometimes slept in one of his T-shirts. Even though it was clean it smelled of him, you know? That was before I stopped liking him, of course."

I nodded. Should I ask if she'd started liking him again? Better not.

It was kind of pally, sitting with her like this. I was almost enjoying it. Almost forgetting why we were sitting here in the first place.

She sighed. "Okay. I think I'm ready to go to sleep now."

"Oh, no, you're not. That's not the point of this. YOU MUST NOT SLEEP."

"Right. Absolutely. I won't."

I gave her Grandma's cell phone number, gathered my comforter around me, took my clock, and stood up. "Maybe I'll set my alarm for five and come get you. Remember, if he comes down those stairs wait till he goes out the door, then run up and get me. First door on the right."

"I'm there." She shivered and pulled her quilt tighter around her.

I started for the stairs.

"You really think some guys would think I'm okay-looking?" she whispered after me.

"They might," I said. "Who knows?"

I went quietly up the stairs and into my room, all pumped up now. I decided I'd write a bit in my mystery notebook, make myself some notes. Pretty soon I'd be weaving a story out of all that had happened and anything that would happen from now to the end. That would be the climax of the story. The crisis came first and was the part where the hero had to decide which way to turn, what to do next. I had a feeling the crisis and the climax were almost here.

I opened the notebook and spread out my map one more time. Here we were at the Lazy Y Ranch. I finger-traced my way up tomorrow's route, which in some places overlapped the Big C, and then I stopped, my heart pounding against my rib cage.

Oh my gosh!

Of course.

That's what he was after. I knew it for sure. His mission.

Tomorrow would be the crisis.

Tomorrow night, the climax.

I went down to tell Geneva. There was no way I could sleep.

★ ★ ★

CHAPTER

16

★ ★ ★

In the morning I was woozy and fuzzy. Not enough sleep again. I sat in the bus with Grandma. Sometimes I'd look back at Geneva and her dad. She was dozing, her head on her dad's shoulder, her fingers playing with the turquoise butterfly on its chain.

"We're going to see some of the world's biggest sculptures today, carved right into the face of the mountain," Declan said. He was wearing a flag shirt, Old Glory, the stripes and stars marching across his chest and back. In honor, I guess, of what we were to see. "One of the sculptures is still a work in progress," he went on. "A gigantic carving of Crazy Horse, great chief of the Oglala Sioux. Crazy Horse led the Sioux and Cheyenne in the Battle of the Little Bighorn, where Lieutenant Colonel George Custer and his command were wiped out. The carving of the chief on his horse will be six hundred forty-one feet long and five hundred sixty-three feet high when it's completed. But first"—he paused—"Mount Rushmore."

I looked to the left and saw Stavros. He was clutching the red bag so tightly that the knuckles of his unbandaged hand were white and shiny. Oh, yes, Mr. Stavros. *This* is what you've been waiting for.

"Mount Rushmore," Declan repeated. "I defy anyone on this bus to be unmoved when we first catch a glimpse of the heads of four of our most famous presidents: George Washington, Thomas Jefferson, Theodore Roosevelt, and Abraham Lincoln, carved so powerfully into the rock. We will spend this afternoon at Mount Rushmore. Tonight we'll stay in a delightful little motel in a small town called Hill City, only a few miles from the monument. You will find all kinds of information about the carvings in the museum, right in the park. But I thought I'd fill you in a little bit before we get there."

He went on to tell us about the sculptor Gutzon Borglum, who'd had a vision of a national monument hewn out of the mass of rock known as Mount Rushmore. The words and faces of the four chosen presidents would be "carved high, as close to heaven as we can."

"It was quite a job," Declan added. "I like to say it was accomplished with drills and dynamite and dreams."

As Declan talked, I watched Stavros. I could only see the side of his face as he stared straight at Declan, concentrating on every word. What was he thinking? That he could turn those dreams into rubble? That there'd be a gigantic boom and the four leaders of America would be gone? Almost as good as blowing up the Statue of Liberty. Or the World Trade Center. And his name would be hated by us and admired by other terrorists.

I was suddenly too hot, boiling hot, steaming hot, sweating inside my jacket. Who did I think *I* was to stop him? Too risky. Way too risky.

I eyed Declan. No good. I'd tried him before. What if I whispered to the Texans, and to Buffo, and to Geneva's dad and Mr. Dove, and—oh, yes—Millie? "He's going to blow up the monument." What if we rushed Stavros the way the guys in the plane had rushed the hijackers? They wouldn't believe me. What proof of anything did I have? None. It sounded too outrageous. Millie would believe me. She'd want to. But suppose, suppose, suppose I was wrong? No, Geneva and I were on our own. I glanced up at the paper-wrapped shovel. What if I stole it as we were getting out of the bus? Would that stop him?

We were driving up a winding road. Wildflowers bloomed on either side. Ponderosa pines swayed in a little breeze. The Black Hills of South Dakota surrounded us. Someone shouted, "Eagle!" and I looked up and out and there it was, circling overhead, so magnificent, so calm, so in its own place.

"You are in the sacred land of the Sioux, almost unchanged since the beginning of time," Declan said softly.

And then Scotty slowed the bus and Declan said, "Gutzon Borglum prophesied, 'American history

shall march along that skyline.' Ladies and gentlemen, there it is."

There was total silence as we saw for the first time
the four great carved faces on Mount Rushmore.

Grandma stopped knitting.

She leaned over and kissed the top of my head,
something she never does in public.

"Makes you proud to be an American, now don't
it?" Buffo asked in a gravelly voice.

Charles Stavros sat, unmoved.

CHAPTER

17

We walked along a wide pathway, lined on both sides with the flags of all the states in the Union. Ahead of us, pushing against the blue prairie sky, were the sculpted heads of the four remembered presidents. I know in ordinary circumstances I would have had that lump in my throat, but I didn't have time to be sentimental or patriotic. I wasn't looking at them, I was looking at Charles Stavros. And I was seeing something different. Today he had a camera. In all of the trip so far I hadn't seen a camera in his hand. I hadn't seen him take a single picture. Today he was taking a lot. He'd stop, set the red bag between his feet, focus, and click. It was a Polaroid camera and he'd stand with one picture in his hand for a few seconds waiting for it to process. Then he'd slide it into an envelope and slip that into his pocket.

He's in a hurry to view them, I thought. I imagined him in his motel room later, the photographs lined up on top of his dresser, choosing his spot. How creepy was that?

I took a deep breath.

A bighorn sheep was climbing an outcropping of rock. Midge stopped to quickly sketch it. Tourists took pictures. Stavros strode on. He wasn't interested in bighorn sheep, just in Mount Rushmore. I saw him turn so he could get a picture of the wooden paths that wound around and far below the gray stone heads. My throat went tight. He was casing the area, finding the best place to stash the bomb, photographing, getting ready. He wouldn't try anything now in daylight, bright sunshine streaming down.

Along the pathway, uniformed rangers spoke into their walkie-talkies, answered questions from the tourists.

Not now. I remembered the flashlight. He'd be back.

Declan had told us to enjoy, to walk up as far as we were allowed, to visit the shops and the museum and the amphitheater.

"You mean we can't actually climb *on* the heads?" Blessing sounded put out.

Declan smiled a superior smile. "Definitely not. The only ones who can climb up there are the animals. And of course the workmen who keep the sculptures in good shape. They use scaffolding and swing them-selves down on ropes when they have to make repairs. Winters are brutal up here and there are always cracks to fill in." He reached out and tweaked Geneva's nose. "Thomas Jefferson needed a nose job a couple of years back. He didn't complain a bit."

Geneva glared up at him. "Hey, buddy!" she said. "I'm complaining. Leave my nose out of it."

Declan grinned. "Sorry, ma'am!"

We gathered around him on the big flagstone patio below the monument. "I want to get a group picture," he said. "If you could all stand by the wall . . ."

We stood. The four Texans knelt in front.

Millie and Beth were next to me. "Let's see Stavros hide himself in *this* picture," Millie whispered to me. "Too late now to send it back home, but I'll get him later. No kidding. There'll be no way to hide from the FBI. They can trace him."

"Too late," she'd said. She didn't even know how late that could be.

I watched him stand at the end of the line, squinting into the sun, and I thought that was one of the scariest things of all. He didn't mind having his picture taken now. Why? Because there was no one to stop him now. Only Geneva and me. And he didn't even know about us.

"Say 'sweet,' everyone," Declan ordered, and we chorused it together as his camera clicked.

"Bee-utiful!" He held up a hand. His star-spangled-banner shirt looked just right in this setting. "I'd like to meet back here at four o'clock. We'll go see the Crazy Horse Monument and then on to our motel.

It's very close, so if anyone wants another visit tomorrow before we leave for Rapid City, I'm sure Scotty will be willing to take you."

It was hard to look at Geneva, who was looking at me. Tomorrow! Would there even be a tomorrow for Mount Rushmore?

Our group split up.

I knew I was finally in one of the most remarkable places in America. I knew Grandma was reliving the time she'd been here with Grandpa. I knew this was one of the main reasons she'd brought me, to share in this, to feel the inspiration of it, and I really tried. But my mind kept screaming back to Stavros. Was there anything, *anything* I could do to stop him? Last night I'd thought about how the crisis came toward the end of a story. This was probably it. Close to the end, and for sure I didn't know what to do.

Grandma put an arm loosely around my shoulders. "This is part of your heritage, Kevin. The heritage of all Americans.'"

I nodded and the lump in my throat came anyway.

Grandma decided she wanted a cup of coffee, and she and Midge sat at one of the small outdoor tables.

Soon most of the others had joined them. Geneva and I got ice-cream cones and leaned across the wall, looking up at the granite faces, so lifelike, so incredible. I'd seen pictures of the Sphinx of Egypt and I could tell it wasn't any greater than these guys! Declan had told us how, during construction, drillers had bored holes in the rock and pushed in dynamite. As they neared the finish of the faces, the eyes and the cheeks and the chins were chiseled out with air tools. It seemed impossible.

Awesome.

I liked it that Geneva was quiet beside me.

"There's no way he can get up there to blow up those faces," she said at last. "I didn't think they'd be so high. It's like they're carved on top of Mount Everest."

"I know. Maybe he's going to bomb the observation deck. I saw him take a picture of it."

"That wouldn't be worth anything. The deck could be fixed. But if he destroyed the heads the whole mountain would come down. And the four presidents would be gone forever."

I dumped the end of my cone in a trash can and

leaned my head on my arms, staring up. A mist had begun to creep up over the mountain, making the shrouded figures above us even more mysterious. Geneva was right. There would be no way to get up there.

How was he going to do it?

Beside us a ranger was talking to a group of Japanese tourists. Everything he said in English an interpreter repeated in Japanese.

"George Washington was the first president to be sculpted. But Abraham Lincoln was Borglum's favorite because he had held our country together during the Civil War. That is why many people think Lincoln's is the best-defined portrait on Mount Rushmore."

There were nods all around.

"We've got to tell," I told Geneva. "We've got to."

No use trying to explain any of this to one of the rangers. Too weird and too vague. The locked red bag that Stavros talked to; the hiding his face from photographs; the way he kept to himself, wouldn't talk, took the bag everywhere; his conversation with the doctor in Cody. The shovel, the flashlight. They'd think he was a little strange, that's all. They'd think *I* was a little strange.

"We have to make one of the rangers look in Stavros's bag," I said to Geneva. "That will convince them. Then it's up to them. Is that cool with you?"

After all, she'd been part of this almost from the beginning. It was only fair that she should have a say in the way it would end.

Geneva nodded. "I think it's too risky for us to do by ourselves. All along I thought we could. But now, when it's about to happen . . ."

I stuck out my hand and she shook it.

"Pact," I said.

"Pact."

But even as we agreed, and even though I knew this was the right thing to do, I was disappointed. Heroes didn't do this. Saint George was supposed to slay his own dragon and I was passing the sword to somebody else. But the stakes were too big.

I waited till the interpreter was interpreting a long, long sentence and then I touched the ranger's arm. "There's something I have to tell you. It's urgent. See that man over there? He's got something—something dangerous—in his bag."

The interpreter's voice faltered. She glanced at me, then went on hesitantly. I knew she'd heard.

The ranger took my arm. He had a red, round face and a bushy mustache. His ears stuck out. Dark sunglasses hid his eyes.

"Excuse me," he said to the Japanese group, and he pulled me a little away. Geneva came, too.

"What do you mean, dangerous? Do you have information that he's carrying drugs?"

I stared up at him. Drugs! I'd never thought of that.

"Was he trying to sell? To you? To the girl?"

"No." I shook my head and then wished I'd said yes, because then for sure he'd have checked out that bag.

"Then what?" He was staring over at Stavros, who was sitting at a table alone, reading one of the Mount Rushmore pamphlets. The ranger's grip on my arm tightened. "Does he have a gun?"

"I don't think so. But I don't know."

I looked to Geneva for help. She didn't give me any.

"What, then? I hope you don't think this is some kind of joke?"

"We know it's not a joke," I blurted. "We've been watching him since the first day of our trip. He's going to do something really bad." Oh, man! No way did I sound like a detective. More like a whiny kid. Which I'm not.

The ranger took off his sunglasses, I guess so he could inspect us more closely. "Are you making this up to get back at him for something?"

He was still holding my arm as if he truly was going to drag me off to the nearest prison.

"Just take him somewhere and open the bag," I said desperately. "Please. See for yourself."

The ranger pulled down his uniform jacket and put his sunglasses back on.

"Okay. The two of you stay here. Don't move. You made a report to me. I guess I have to follow through."

We watched him walk toward Stavros.

"He doesn't believe us," Geneva said. "It's because we're kids. Nobody takes kids seriously."

I took a deep breath. "Think how he'd have been if we'd told him about the bomb. I think we took the right course of action."

We saw him stop by Stavros and point to the bag.

Stavros stood and the two of them walked toward a building close to the gift shop. They disappeared inside.

"If he does find—," Geneva began, then corrected herself. "*When* he does find the bomb, we have to be sure we get credit—"

"Oh puh-lease," I said. "Get over yourself!"

We paced across the patio and back. "Will he take Stavros—," Geneva began, and then said, "Uh-oh, here they come."

Stavros and the ranger came out of the building. They were talking in an okay way, not as if one of them was a cop and the other his prisoner. There were no handcuffs, no gun.

My stomach lurched.

"I don't think he found the bomb," Geneva whispered. "What did Stavros do with it? He must have hidden it someplace around here."

"No way," I said. "I watched him every minute."

Stavros sat again at the table where he'd been before. The pamphlet he'd been reading was still there. So was his glass of lemonade. I couldn't tell by looking at him if he was angry or not. Maybe he was used to being searched because of the way he looked. Maybe he was always pulled out of the security line at the airport. He must hate it. Still, that was what security was for. I wasn't going to start feeling sorry for him. I couldn't wait for the ranger to come and tell us what he'd found in the bag and when he'd arrest Stavros.

He didn't come to us directly, which I thought was smart. You should never do that when an informant had informed. It's a giveaway. There might be retaliation. That was a theory from my mystery-writing book.

After a few minutes he came over, stopped on the way to speak to a man and woman, pointed out something to them on a map, then leaned on the wall beside us.

"I should give you two a citation," he said coldly. "One thing I hate is to be guilty of discrimination. And I have to ask myself if I would have paid any attention to what you said if Mr. Stavros had looked different. That doesn't make me feel so great about myself."

I felt myself cower as I looked up at him. His face was redder than ever.

"Yes, sir," Geneva said. "But about the bag? Could we ask what's in it?"

"You could not." He looked so fierce, I took a step back. "What's in there is none of your business. Now be good kids and go back to your parents and give this a rest. You can be grateful that I have teenagers of my own who sometimes get themselves into stupid situations. Though if they ever pulled something like this, I'd tan their hides."

"Yes, sir," I said.

It was more than a relief when he turned and walked away. Thank goodness he hadn't demanded to talk to Grandma. That would really have been bad.

"What do you think?" I'd never heard Geneva's voice so small and shaky.

"I still think he has a bomb. He must have hidden it somewhere. Maybe he remembered how many rangers would be hanging around."

"But what about 'I'll never let you go again?'" Geneva whispered.

"I don't know. But I think he's going to do it

tonight," I said, surprised at how strong and tough I sounded. My detective instincts had taken over again, big time. "And I think now we're the only ones who can stop him."

★ ★ ★

CHAPTER

18

★ ★ ★

He went that night.

I'd already figured out how he was going to get back to Mount Rushmore and how we could follow him.

Our motel was long and L-shaped. All the doors and windows faced the parking lot. There was an upstairs and a downstairs. The Star Tours people were booked in the lower level.

As soon as Scotty drove us in I saw the bicycles. They were in a rack. There would have been six of them, but two were out when we parked. I saw

Charles Stavros eye them. He walked over to the rack, pulled one out, examined it, put it back, and asked Declan, "Are these for us?"

"For any of the guests to use. Enjoy!" Declan said.

It was three miles back along the road to Mount Rushmore. Not a hard walk. But a bike would make it even easier.

I was thinking logically, which was strange. It was almost as if, now that the time had come, I was ready. Except . . .

"Geneva," I said. "You have to be the watcher. It won't be dark for at least two hours and I have to sleep. I don't think anything's going to happen while it's daylight. And this is perfect. You can see his door from the window of your room. It won't be hard at all."

She didn't argue. "Okay," she said. "But only two hours. Set your alarm."

Oh, that bed! It felt as good as it looked. When the buzzer went off I staggered outside, blinking in the sunlight. "More sleep, more sleep!" my brain screamed. "When all this is over," I promised it.

Geneva burst out of her room. "I thought you

were never getting up," she grumbled. "I'm so bored with staring at those parked cars. I memorized all the license numbers, if you want to know how bored I was. And it was a waste of time. Stavros never appeared."

I raised my eyebrows. "You'd have liked it more if he had?"

She gave me one of her famous looks.

"We have to make plans," I said.

We sat on one of the green wooden benches outside our rooms.

Geneva had borrowed her dad's cell phone. I had Grandma's.

"Is this really going to happen?" Geneva asked. "It's as if we've been playacting all this time. You know, making it up as we went along. And now . . . I still think it's a game."

She was wearing the rodeo cap, turned backward, a navy blue sweatshirt that said JACKSON LAKE and exactly matched her fake eyes, baggy jeans, and running shoes. And the butterfly necklace. I had a feeling she'd never take that off.

Charles Stavros came out of his room then and I

stiffened. But he just looked up at the sky and went back inside.

"Checking the weather," I whispered to Geneva and shivered, even though it wasn't cold. I leaned back against the hard bench and concentrated on not drifting off to sleep. In books, detectives never seem to sleep. Maybe a person needs practice not sleeping.

Geneva was messing around with the phone, making the dial light up, turning it off again.

"Did your dad mind lending it?" I asked. "What did you tell him?"

"That you and I wanted to talk, room to room. Don't worry. He didn't make any Declan kind of remark."

I nodded, then asked, "Do you like him better now than at the beginning? Your dad?"

"Yep," she said.

"Was it your mom who kind of turned you against him?"

"Hey!" She sat up straight. "Don't you go dissing my mom!"

"I'm not. I just wondered."

She didn't look at me or say anything else and I

could tell I'd guessed right, even if she didn't want to say.

I kept watching Stavros's door. It was going to be dark soon. TV sets flickered inside rooms. I could see odd movements through Buffo and Blessing's window and it took a while to realize they were doing floor exercises, popping up into view and then disappearing, like puppets in a shadow box.

The Doves' drapes were closed.

So were Stavros's.

"What time do you think he'll go?" Geneva asked.

"When it's really dark."

"Kev? Do we know what we're going to do when we catch him with the bomb?"

"Definitely." I sounded surer than I was. "First we'll rush him and knock him out before he can do anything. Then we'll call 911."

"How are we going to knock him out? He's big."

"Don't worry about it," I said. "I have a plan."

Geneva stared hard at me. "Don't you tell me not to worry in that kind of a voice! It's like giving me a pat on the head. I'm in this as much as you are. I hate it when I'm patronized. Don't you dare do it!"

"Sorry," I mumbled.

The light was almost gone. A fan of birds, chirping and calling to each other, hurried home to their nests. Little points of light sparked here and there. I wondered if they were fireflies. I wondered if they had fireflies in South Dakota. There was no breeze, but I was shivering again.

"I wish that ranger had found the bomb," Geneva said. "I mean, how can you miss a bomb?"

"You're thinking of something huge. Bombs can be little now. No bigger than a cell phone. Or a camera." I paused. "Besides, we figured he must have hidden it somewhere."

"I thought you said it was big and bulky," Geneva muttered.

"They can be any size," I said with authority. "It doesn't matter. Either kind works."

He went at midnight. The witching hour. I was spying from my window and I saw him come out his door, carrying the red bag and the shovel, still in its wrappings. It was fully dark, but there were lights in the parking lot and a bright three-quarter moon that was like a yellow scoop in the sky.

I dialed frantically. My fingers didn't want to work on the small keys of the cell. Geneva wasn't answering and wasn't answering.

"C'mon, c'mon!" I muttered.

She was asleep. I knew it. She was going to blow the whole thing. I didn't want to do this alone. Why couldn't she have stayed up on this night of all nights?

And then I heard her voice, fully awake, scared. "Kevin?"

"He's going. Wait till he rides out of the driveway."

I watched him from my darkened room as he took the bike he'd looked at before, hung the red bag from its handlebars, and balanced the shovel across them.

My backpack was ready. The only things in it were my flashlight and the glass globe that I'd bought for my mom in the Jackson Lake Lodge gift shop. The globe was heavy. Inside it was an image of the snow-topped Tetons, and when you shook it, snowflakes swirled around. Would I have the guts to use it, to crack Stavros over the head with it? In all the mystery stories I'd read, the detective had never, that

I could remember, used a snow globe for a weapon. But a detective has to be flexible and use whatever is available.

I saw Geneva's door open, and I opened mine and closed it quietly behind me. In the connecting room next to mine, Grandma was asleep. I hoped.

Geneva and I met at the bike racks. Carefully, carefully we lifted two bikes to the ground, not speaking, everything going as we had planned.

There were no lights at the front of our bikes, or his. Not that any of us would have switched one on. But at the back, on the wheels, were red lights that turned and turned as you pedaled. We could see his, quite a bit in front of us.

The sky was black. The scoop of moon, partly covered by drifts of clouds, came and disappeared. On either side of us, bushes whispered and rustled. What was in there? Bears? No, probably just deer. Hopefully deer.

One mile.

Two. Three.

"Look!" Geneva breathed, and in a flare of moonlight I saw the four heads silhouetted against the sky. Washington, Jefferson, Roosevelt, Lincoln. I had a sudden memory of first grade, making silhouettes of ourselves with black paper, gluing them onto white paper, taking them home. Mom hugging me. "Oh, Kevin! It's you!"

I was breaking up, getting jumpier every minute. *Stop it, Kevin. Just stop it.*

Ahead of us, the red lights stopped moving.

"Kev?" Geneva whispered.

"Shh."

We slid off our bikes and laid them silently at the side of the road. To our left was a pasture. There was the faraway glint of black water. Everywhere I looked there were mountains, the Black Hills of South Dakota. The Badlands were there, too, not far away, and drifting against the night sky were the four American presidents that Charles Stavros had come to destroy.

About fifty feet ahead of us a flashlight went on.

"Down," I whispered.

We threw ourselves on our stomachs on the road.

I raised my head, just a little, and saw him squeeze

through the sparse bushes into a dirt field. His flashlight was the kind that's also a lantern. Push once for the flashlight part, push twice and you had a small fluorescent lamp. Stavros had set it beside him. The red bag was open next to him. With his good hand he was unwrapping the shovel, unfolding the handle.

We lay there beside the trunk of an old fallen tree, as still as the tree itself.

The night silence was broken by the sluff and scuffle of a shovel turning over earth. Moonlight silvered the small tufts of grass.

"Now," I whispered. "We have to stop him now."

We went on all fours, hugging the ground, closing the gap. My almost-empty backpack flapped against my shoulders. Pebbles jabbed at my hands. Geneva was a little behind me. I could hear her breath, little raspy grunts, and I wanted to whisper, "Be quieter, can't you?" But I knew I was probably breathing the same way. We dropped prone and watched.

He was about twenty yards ahead of us now. How long would it take us to reach him? It was like the old school problem: "If a train leaves the station . . ."

Stop it, Kevin. Concentrate. Slay the dragon.

I shrugged off my backpack, eased it to the ground, unzipped it a little, careful of the noise. The glass globe! That's all I would need.

"Stay here and call 911," I whispered.

"No."

"Yes."

I stood, realizing that Geneva was beside me and that we were both running toward him, blundering through the bushes.

"Hey!" I shouted. "What do you think you're doing?"

He was on his knees and he'd lifted something from the bag and was lowering it into the hole he'd dug.

"Stop!" I roared.

"Give up, you're surrounded!" Geneva yelled.

I saw his startled face. I saw his hands, covered with loose earth, lift out of the hole. The element of surprise, I thought.

Surprise, surprise, surprise.

I almost shouted it. Instead I raised the snow globe of the Tetons.

The snowflakes inside danced and glittered in the lantern light.

At the top of the arc, at the release point for a pitcher, I stuttered to a stop. His face was turned up to me. How could I smash this down on anybody's face, even if he was a terrorist?

I couldn't.

"Get him," I yelled at Geneva and the two of us threw ourselves on top of him. The lantern was knocked over. He was grunting, saying, "What the—" and then, "Kevin? You followed me? What . . . ?"

We were rolling over together, the three of us.

"Grab his arm," I shouted. I had his bandaged one, but I wouldn't be able to hold on to it for long. I sat on his head.

His legs scissored and kicked.

"Ouch!" Geneva said.

"We need to—" I panted. "We need to tie him up." But I hadn't thought of that. I'd only thought of knocking him out. We had no rope. Nothing.

He had wriggled free, and in the light from the tumbled-over lantern he was standing over us now, massive, dark, terrifying.

"Are you kids crazy?" But there was a shakiness in his voice. "Who else is with you?" he asked, peering into the darkness.

Never admit you're alone. I didn't know if I'd read that or just knew it.

"Everybody," I said quickly, and Geneva said again, "Give up, you're surrounded."

He listened. So did we. Nothing but silence, not even the sounds of the animals. We'd scared them into silence. I looked up and there were the presidents, way, way above us, maybe a mile away, still, impassive, ageless, mysterious.

I'm doing this for you, I told them silently.

"You thought you were going to blow up those guys." I pointed with a trembling hand.

"No way," Geneva said. Her voice quivered.

"What do you mean, blow them up?" Stavros took a step toward the red bag. Oh my gosh! What if he did have a gun in there? He put his hand inside it.

I tried to stand in front of Geneva but she shoved me away. She was dialing the phone, saying, "Drat, drat." And then her shoulders slumped. "There's no signal."

The mountains, I thought. Of course there's no signal. Why didn't we think of that?

"Run," I yelled, and I knew I should run, too, but I couldn't.

We stood, frozen in time, staring at what Stavros had taken from the bag. "It's a boot," I whispered. A boot! How could that be?

"Yes. The other one's already in the hole," Stavros said.

"The bomb's in a boot?" Geneva asked incredulously.

Stavros turned to us. "No bomb. Come on! Did you really think I had a bomb?

"You've been carrying those two old boots around all this time?" My voice rose to a squeak. Dull, worn, black. Old, misshapen. Two boots. *That's* why the bag had been so heavy.

"They were my father's," Stavros said as if that explained everything.

"But . . . why?"

He didn't answer. Instead he bent and gently lowered the boot into the hole with the other. He spaded the loose dirt on top, then crouched and patted the earth smooth. His head was bent, his eyes closed. It was as if we weren't there. I could knock him out now if I wanted. He wouldn't even see me coming. But . . . I had this strong feeling that he was praying, or maybe not.

Neither Geneva nor I spoke.

It was so weird, here in the dark, the lantern shining around our feet as we stood in silence, the moon fringing the edges of the clouds, the presidents above, listening. Even though I knew we might still be in danger, even though things could go from here to worse, the writer in me saw the scene and filed it away for a story setting. I guess writers never turn themselves off.

He made the sign of the cross over the small mound and I remembered how he'd done that, the first day, on the bus.

He stood and I heard him take a deep, raggedy breath.

"All right," he said, and the way he said it made me know that he'd come to a decision. "I'll tell you."

He didn't look at us.

"I'm a fireman," he went on. "My father was, too.

We didn't work together much, but we were together on the day of September eleventh, 2001. In the Twin Towers. Every firefighter in the city was there that day. Even the older guys." He stopped, coughed, moved a little. "My father died. The fire burned through . . ."

"Oh!" Geneva took a step toward him as if she was going to hug him. "I'm so so so sorry!" I don't know if he heard her or saw her.

"I was pulling him up. I had his arm, the fire came in a sweep from below." He stopped again. "I let go." He paused. "The media got it, of course. Newspapers. TV. Two heroes, father and son. One died."

That's where Millie saw his picture, I thought, and at the same time I realized that he was standing so he could see the presidents' heads against the faraway sky and that he seemed to be talking to them, not to us at all.

"My father loved this country," he went on. "He'd been here at Mount Rushmore twice. He joked that he wanted to be buried here, with the presidents watching over him for all time." Stavros touched the little mound gently with his toe. "These boots, his spare boots, were a part of him. The fire took the ones he wore, along with everything else."

He leaned down and switched off the lantern.

"We thought," I said into the darkness, "we thought . . ."

"Sometimes since nine-eleven people do."

"We're sorry that we thought that way. Just because . . ."

Stavros nodded.

Geneva and I hovered, not knowing what to say or do next.

"Did you hurt your hand in the fire?" Geneva asked, sounding polite and ordinary.

"No. I was careless with a saw in my workshop. I had planned on driving out here. But the accident put a stop to that."

"That must have hurt," Geneva said.

I couldn't believe her with her small talk.

"I think we should go back now," I said to her. And then to Stavros, "I don't suppose you want to come yet?"

"I'll stay for a while," he said, and then dopey Geneva added, "Don't forget to pick up your wrapping paper. We don't litter."

I thought Stavros smiled.

I didn't look back at him once as we went for our bikes.

This little bit of time for him was private and precious.

CHAPTER

19

★ ★ ★

We left the next day for Rapid City, South Dakota. We'd stay the night in the old Alex Johnson Hotel there, then catch our flights home. Geneva and I exchanged e-mail addresses. I might write to her if I have nothing better to do. I probably will. Only because I'll probably never meet another girl with fake eyes and yellow hair. Who's brave, too.

I was surprised at how hard it was to say last good-byes. At the beginning Declan had told us we should get pally and I'd thought, Come on! That'll never happen on a bus tour. But it had happened. I'd miss everyone, even Millie. Well, not so much Millie.

She whispered to me that she'd be staying on the trail of Stavros when she got back. "I won't give up," she said.

I shrugged. "Good luck." I wasn't about to tell her his private and precious secret.

Stavros waved to Geneva and me as we left the bus for the last time. The red bag, light now, swung from his hand. The new bandage was streaked with dirt.

"Say hello to Sunshine for me," Midge told him.

"I will. Thanks."

"Bye," we said. "Bye, Mr. Stavros."

"He was so *nice*." Geneva giggled.

"And we were jerks," I said.

Geneva gave me one of her high-and-mighty looks. "Maybe *you* were a jerk. I was just doing my patriotic duty."

Oh, brother!

"Here, Mr. Stavros," Grandma said. "I want you to have this as a memento of our trip." She gave him the finished blue scarf. "I'll knit another one for your dad," she told me.

Charles Stavros knotted the scarf around his neck,

then leaned down and gently kissed her cheek. "Thank you," he said.

I wondered what Grandma knew. Probably nothing. But she senses things. That's another one of her talents.

On the plane home the next morning she told me she'd loved this trip and we should plan another one for next summer vacation, which will be all right with me.

I've been catching up on everything in my mystery notebook. I bet I have a story here when I put it all together. One thing pleases me a lot. My how-to-write-a-mystery book says that the first clue presented should be the last one resolved, and in my real-life mystery, that's how it went. First off, I was suspicious of what was in that bag, and that's what I found out last. Okay! Joan Lowery Nixon would be proud of me. Also, in a book, the main character should learn something about himself or the world around him. I'd definitely done that. I think it's okay in a book for a writer to have imagination and think someone's who he isn't. I mean, you've got to have suspense. But I'll remember in real life to be more careful. I think I'll use my original title, though. *The Man with the Red Bag*. In writing we call this "finding an edgy title that will catch the reader and never let go."

So it's over.

But when I lie in bed at night, my head on my familiar, friendly blankey square, I think about that small mound up there in South Dakota, that memorial to a fireman who died. And I think of the four presidents watching over it with love and gratitude.

Maybe that's just the writer in me, being romantic and imaginative.

But anyway, that's what I think.